CHRISTMAS

BOOK TWO OF THE CHRISTMAS CARD SERIES

A Novella By

Amanda Tru

Published by
Olivia Kimbrell Press™

Olivia Kimbrell Press™

Copyright Notice

A Cinderella Christmas: Book 2 of the Christmas Card Series

Copyright © 2018 by Amanda Tru. All rights reserved. No part of this publication may be reproduced or transmitted in any form or by any means — electronic, mechanical, photocopying, or recording — without express written permission of the author. The only exception is brief quotations in printed or broadcasted critical articles and reviews.

This book is a work of fiction. Names, characters, places, and incidents are either the product of the author's imagination or are used fictitiously. Any resemblance to actual events, organizations, places, locales or to persons, living or dead, is purely coincidental and beyond the intent of either the author or publisher. The characters are productions of the author's imagination and used fictitiously.

PUBLISHED BY: Olivia Kimbrell Press™*, P.O. Box 470, Fort Knox, KY 40121-0470. The Olivia Kimbrell Press™ colophon and open book logo are trademarks of Olivia Kimbrell Press™.

*Olivia Kimbrell Press™ is a publisher offering true to life, meaningful fiction from a Christian worldview intended to uplift the heart and engage the mind.

Some scripture quotations courtesy of the King James Version (KJV) of the Holy Bible. Some scripture quotations courtesy of the New King James Version (NKJV) of the Holy Bible, Copyright© 1979, 1980, 1982 by Thomas-Nelson, Inc. Used by permission. All rights reserved.

Cover Design and Title Graphics by Chautona Havig

Library Cataloging Data

Names: Tru, Amanda (Amanda Tru) 1978-

Title: A Cinderella Christmas; Book 2 of the Christmas Card series / Amanda Tru

234 p. 5 in. × 8 in. (12.70 cm × 20.32 cm)

Description: Olivia Kimbrell Press™ digital eBook edition | Olivia Kimbrell Press™ Trade paperback edition | Kentucky: Olivia Kimbrell Press™, 2018.

Summary: A notebook meant to heal one heart, inspires the hearts of many.

Identifiers: ePCN: 2018963358 | ISBN-13: 978-1-68190-138-1 (ebk.) | 978-1-68190-139-8 (POD) | 978-1-68190-140-4 (trade) | 978-1-68190-141-1 (hardcover)

1. clean romance love story 2. women's inspirational 3. man woman relationships 4. Christian living 5. Christmas Card book 6. based on a true story 7. holiday season couple

A Cinderella CHRISTMAS

BOOK TWO OF THE CHRISTMAS CARD SERIES

A Novella By

Table of Contents

A Cinderella Christmas 1
    Table of Contents 4
    Dedication 6
Prologue 7
Chapter 1 17
Chapter 2 25
Chapter 3 33
Chapter 4 45
Chapter 5 53
Chapter 6 63
Chapter 7 71
Chapter 8 79
Chapter 9 89
Chapter 10 99
Chapter 11 111
Chapter 12 121
Chapter 13 129

Chapter 14	143
Chapter 15	151
Chapter 16	159
Chapter 17	169
Chapter 18	179
Chapter 19	191
Epilogue	201
Author's Note	216
Reader's Guide	219
Excerpt from Under the Christmas Star	224
More Great Books by Amanda Tru	231
About Amanda Tru	234

Dedication

TO Him who could have prevented it all and didn't. May You be glorified in all my even ifs.

2 Corinthians 1:3-4

Prologue

THE car in front of me continues into the intersection, not stopping before completing the left turn. Glancing up at the green light, I smoothly follow the other car in my own turn. As my SUV rounds the corner, I glance up at the light again.

Shock and fear jolt my body like electricity.

The light is not green. Instead, a flashing yellow light blinks an arrow.

I can't breathe.

My mind races, cramming calculations into the space of a split second. Do I hit the brakes? But it's too late! I'm half-way through the intersection. Should I hit the gas?

I catch movement out of the corner of my eye. A strangled shriek leaps from my throat.

Before my mind tells me what it is, my hands wrench the wheel, but there is nowhere to escape.

Then, the impact.

My body lurches with the car, but it feels like hitting a large curb or speed bump. There's no crash of glass. No airbag in my face.

I blink. My breath sucks in with a rush and my hands jerk

in violently—but they are the only things moving in the sudden stillness

You're okay. It isn't that bad. It's just a fender bender. Not that bad.

I lean forward, trying to catch a glimpse of the car I never actually saw before it impacted my front wheel. It is tiny, tucking perfectly into my blind spot at the front passenger side of my small SUV.

The last two seconds didn't happen. It didn't happen. You're Ok.

I see a woman in the front seat. I see her move.

Relieved, I take another breath.

The other driver is ok. It'll be fine. Just a fender bender. You're ok.

I need to get out of the intersection.

I need to get my vehicle off the street and pull to the side.

I need to check the other driver and give her my insurance information.

I need to call the police.

I need to rewind the last thirty seconds.

I try to breathe again, but it's just a series of shuddering hiccups as if breathing through a straw.

I push my foot on the gas pedal. The engine revs but the car doesn't move.

I shift into "park." Then back into "drive" and try again. It still won't move.

I look helplessly at the cars surrounding me in the intersection. Everyone is staring, but no one is really looking at me. They are all spectators, trying to figure out a way around the accident.

Shifting it into "park" again, I give up.

I need help.

I unfasten my seatbelt and open my car door. Grabbing my cell phone from the center console, I hurry to the other car.

The woman looks like she's struggling to get out. I open the car door.

"I am so sorry," I say. "Are you hurt?"

"My foot is hurt." She is an older woman. I guess her to be in her late fifties or sixties. She has glasses, and her short hair is a color in between brown and red.

Both airbags in her small vehicle are deployed, and the front part of the car is smashed close to her knees. I don't know if she could get out of the vehicle, even if her foot wasn't hurt.

"Do you need an ambulance?" I ask.

"I don't think I can move," she answered.

I immediately lift my phone, but my fingers shake and sweat so badly that I can barely manage to find the numbers to dial.

"911. What is your emergency?"

"I was just in an accident. The other driver is injured, and we need an ambulance."

"What is your location?"

I automatically look around at the intersection. I know where I am, but the street names can't seem to crawl off my tongue. I find the street signs. "I'm at the corner of Pinehurst and 5th Street."

"What are the vehicles involved in the accident?"

"I have a gray Kia Sorrento, and..." I turn to the other woman. "What car do you drive?"

"A Smart Car," she answered.

"A silver Smart Car," I echo back.

"What are the injuries?"

"She's having pain in her foot." I hear my voice responding to the question as if someone else is speaking. The voice is calm, coherent, and professional. Nothing like the riot of shock and anxiety erupting inside me.

I finish with the operator and hang up. I turn to the woman. "I'm so sorry." I feel tears burning behind my eyes. She is obviously in a lot of pain. And it is all my fault. I feel so very helpless. "Would you mind if I prayed for you?" I ask, grasping onto the only way I know to help.

The woman doesn't respond, which I take as consent.

"Dear, Lord, please help this woman. I feel so sorry for what happened. Ease the pain for her. Help her foot to be alright. Just put your arms around both of us and hold us close. In Jesus' name. Amen."

It wasn't eloquent. I don't even know if it was right. But it is all I could think to do.

You're okay. She has a broken foot but isn't seriously injured. It'll be fine.

"Didn't you see me?" the woman asks.

More sharp tears of guilt slice through me.

"No, I didn't," I respond, my voice shaking with emotion. "I thought the light was green."

We wait for a few more breaths as I watch helplessly. I assume cars in the intersection are maneuvering around us, but no one stops. No passersby come to help, and I'm not really aware of anything beyond the woman in the crumpled car in front of me and the guilt that is already suffocating.

"Help should be here any minute," I soothe. I look around desperately, wishing that promised help would materialize, even though I know it will take several minutes for an ambulance to arrive.

You're okay. It's just a few minutes. They'll come. Help is on its way. She'll be okay.

Though the accident happened in a split-second, I now feel the weight of each full second that slowly passes.

I glance from her vehicle, to mine. While the only damage to my SUV is the front passenger side, her car is crumpled like a soda can. Resembling a toy car, her vehicle had been no match for my SUV. With its entire front smashed, the Smart Car is clearly totaled.

At the sight of the mess, a wave of nausea hits me. I'm in a surreal twilight zone, and my mind keeps screaming an adamant, *This isn't happening!*

Thankfully, I hear the squeal of sirens, and within another thirty seconds, officers arrive and begin taking over.

A mustached officer casually walks up to me and asks, "What happened?"

"It's my fault," I admit bravely. "I was turning left. I thought the light was green, and it was flashing yellow. By the time I realized it, it was too late. I couldn't get away."

Even as I'm calling myself an idiot, I continue my report. I'd heard before that you aren't supposed to admit fault or say anything incriminating after an accident. But how can I not when this was so obviously my fault? If I hadn't read that light wrong, the accident wouldn't have happened, and the other driver wouldn't have been hurt.

It is my fault, and I'm not going to pretend otherwise. *You're okay. Just take responsibility, and it will be fine.*

I watch as the paramedics remove the woman from her car and load her onto a gurney. I flinch as she moans in pain, crying about her foot and now her knee.

Eventually, they load her on the ambulance, and it leaves. I wander around, not sure where to go and what to do. I take out my cell phone and push a few buttons.

'Hi, Mom. It's Emily I was in a car accident." My voice crackles with every word, but I keep my composure. "I'm okay, but it was my fault. My car is being towed, and I need a ride home."

Thankfully, Mom doesn't ask lots of questions. Instead, she asks where I am and says it will be thirty minutes before she can reach me.

"Are you hurt?" a voice asks.

I turn to see the officer I'd spoken to earlier. "No, I'm okay," I reply, automatically repeating the mantra repeating through my brain. Then, in total contradiction, I continue, "My hand hurts." Even as the words come out of my mouth, I'm surprised to realize the pain is radiating from my thumb area. "I think I must have wrenched it when I turned the wheel to try to avoid the accident."

The officer motions to a paramedic. He joins us and asks a few standard questions about the date and our location. He is clearly assessing me for a head injury, though I have no idea why. When I mention my hand, he says that's a common injury and offers to transport me to the hospital if I need to have it checked.

I refuse.

"Do you have a ride?" the officer asks.

"Yes," I nod. "It will just take her a while to get here."

"You can go wait at the corner if you'd like. The tow truck should be here shortly."

I suddenly realize that, of course, I am in the way. I must be in shock. I am aware enough to realize that my mind is not working the way it normally does. Things that should be obvious are not. The officers are busy trying to clean up the accident, and I'm wandering around through the middle of it.

I walk over to the corner, feeling like I'm on a stage with the intersection traffic my audience. Seeing a short cement border around the front lawn of the bank on the corner lot, I sit down and watch.

The accident cleans up rapidly. Tow trucks retrieve both vehicles. A man with a long beard and suspenders comes over and hands me a card with the location of where my SUV will be towed. When he asks what happened, I tell him, again not placing the blame on anyone's shoulders but mine.

He nods, saying that he's seen an awful lot of accidents due to those flashing yellow lights. "I wish they'd just stick with red and green lights. Instead of go or stop, now we have a 'maybe' with a flashing yellow. You have to realize it's a maybe and then check and figure out if the way is clear or not." He shakes his head. "It's just asking for trouble if you ask me."

Then he is gone.

As I watch the glass being swept from the road, the mustached police officer I'd spoken to earlier comes over and sits down beside me. He hands me back my driver's license and registration, though I can't even recall when I'd handed the items to him.

"I have a ticket for you," he said, not without sympathy.

I nod. "I understand."

I look at the ticket made out in carbon duplicate. The top line clearly reads "Emily Jansen," matching the name of the woman with long medium-brown hair standing as if for a mugshot on the front of the driver's license.

"Now this isn't a misdemeanor or anything. I'm just issuing you a ticket for 'failure to yield.' The information you need is all on the ticket here. It gives instructions on either paying the fine or appearing at this court date."

I nod after each phrase he says, appearing that I'm listening and absorbing the information, but the words only swirl around my head and never actually land where they elicit any meaning.

He finishes explaining the details and points to a line that says, "Signature." I sign the ticket, and he tears apart the carbon duplicate, handing me the pink copy.

A humorless laugh escapes my lips at the touch of the thin paper in my hand. "I am thirty years old, and this is the first ticket I've had in my life."

The officer nods. "I encounter people every day, even some older than you, who have accidents and have never gotten a ticket before."

I try to blink back the tears. Knowing that doesn't actually help me in any way.

"I think the other driver will be okay," he said, comfortingly.

My distress must be obvious.

The officer pauses and repeats again. "She may have a long recovery, but I think she'll be okay. Are you sure you have a ride?"

"Yes," I nod bravely. But I lose the battle with my tears. I am now fully sniffling, and heavily-laden moisture escapes from my eyes. "My mom should be here soon."

Relieved, he and all of the other officers leave while I keep my seat on the cement border.

One minute, the intersection is crowded with wrecked cars, tow trucks, and officers directing traffic and cleaning up. The next minute, everything is gone, and traffic is flowing through the intersection as if nothing had happened.

Oh, if I could just believe that nothing had happened!

Tears now stream freely down my face as I cry quietly. My breath catches in little hiccupping sobs, and I watch the intersection as if I can still see the cars smashed against each other. And really, I can. At least, I can see their ghosts.

Over and over, my mind replays the minutes of the accident until now. I repeatedly feel the shock of the impact, the fear of knowing I had hurt someone, and the guilt that accompanies both.

Just make it stop! I beg. I want to go to sleep and wake to find this all a nightmare.

I watch the people walking by. I don't try to fight the emotion anymore. I let the tears fall as an accompaniment to my quiet sobs.

I must look a sight, and yet no one seems to notice. So many people walk past me, their gait slow and relaxed. It's like they don't even see me. They pass on the sidewalk directly in front of where I am perched. If I extended my leg, they would trip over me.

They push the button for the crossing light. Then they stand there and wait. Looking around at the intersection, but never at me. On the signal, the white outline of a person walking lights up, and the pedestrians take off across the street to continue their day.

So many people. I never realized this was such a busy intersection, but it is. Out of the many cars zooming on the street and all the steady stream of people passing me on the sidewalk, no one stops to ask me if I'm okay. No one looks at the girl sobbing on the street corner. No one even slows their steps to check.

I am trapped in a nightmare of my own making. It is my fault. I caused the accident. I hurt someone.

And it could have been worse. What if the other driver had been killed? Even now, what if she was injured worse than it appears?

I've never felt so alone. I try to pray, but every coherent thought is whisked away before it is formed, leaving soft moans of agony in an empty wake. The truth settles in, finally chasing away denial.

I'm not okay.

Yet everyone walks away.

A Cinderella Christmas

Chapter One

Emily

(Six Months Later)

THE bell over the door jingled as Emily pushed open the door. Stepping into the veterinary clinic, she was immediately assaulted by the strong scent of pets and dog food mixed with something medical. It was an aroma distinctive to a vet clinic, and it was one she didn't particularly care for.

Two men were standing to the side of the counter. Emily hesitantly passed them and stepped up to the receptionist.

"My mom sent me to pick up her dog. Her name is Kim Jansen." Emily paused, then added. "That's my mom's name, not the dog's."

The receptionist shot her a withering, impatient smile, as if barely tolerating being bothered. "Please have a seat. We'll get the dog for you."

Feeling as if she'd somehow committed a faux pas, she

ducked her head and retreated to the few plastic chairs lined up against the wall by the door. One of the four chairs was already occupied, so Emily took the one that was farthest away from the man who was busily perusing a fishing magazine.

Not sure how long she'd need to wait, she took a small notebook and pencil from her purse. With the pencil in hand, she opened the tablet to add eggs to her shopping list, but the pencil never met the paper to make a mark.

"The news is not good," a woman in scrubs announced gravely as she emerged from the back recesses of the clinic.

Emily's eyes shot up to see the vet technician addressing the two somber men still standing to the side of the counter. One of the men was tall and wore a baseball cap. Emily guessed his age to be late forties. The other man was considerably older with stooped shoulders and glasses. Emily guessed him to be in his late seventies if not older.

"The dog is in bad shape," the vet tech continued. "He needs surgery if he's going to have a chance to live. The doctor won't know the full damage until he does surgery. But it's bad."

There was a long, tension-filled pause.

"So the dog is fine?" the older man asked.

"No, he isn't fine." the woman said. "It's very serious, and his prognosis will depend on what the doctor finds."

"So he's fine? the man asked again.

It suddenly occurred to Emily that the old man couldn't hear.

"No, he isn't fine," the woman answered again, this time in a very loud voice.

The old man hesitated. "He's going to die?"

"We don't know," she answered loudly. "He needs surgery."

Another long pause.

"I need to know what you want to do," the woman urged.

"It isn't even my dog, it's my daughter's." the younger man said, speaking for the first time. "I was just walking him through the neighborhood when I stopped to talk to this man. He came out of his yard to talk to me and left the gate open. Then his dog ran out through the open gate and attacked my dog. So I'm not sure… "

"I understand," the vet tech said. "But you'll have to work out the details yourself. I just need to know what you want to do. We don't have much time."

"How much will it cost?" the old man asked.

"I don't know. Probably at least $2,000. The doctor doesn't know what he'll find. It could be more, or the dog might not make it."

The old man nodded as if he understood.

The following awkward silence made Emily want to squirm with sheer discomfort. She desperately wanted to get up and comfort the old man. Though the words being spoken were few, a whole lot was being said in between the words. It was clear to Emily what was happening, and it was a horrible situation.

The older man's dog had attacked and injured the dog the younger man was walking and caring for. The younger man clearly expected and wanted the older man to pay for the medical needs of the injured animal. And strictly speaking, he probably should, since it was his dog who had done the damage.

But it was also clear that the older man didn't have the resources to handle a surgery that potentially cost thousands of dollars, and it was also doubtful that he understood or had enough faculties to handle such a decision.

Emily's heart broke for both parties, but mostly for the old man. She longed to get off her chair and put a comforting arm around his stooped, plaid-clad shoulders. She felt so helpless. It wasn't right that the dog's injuries not be cared for, but it also wasn't right that the old man have to pay so much money for a dog that may not even survive after the multi-thousand-dollar cost of trying to save him.

"It's not my dog," the younger man repeated, shifting awkwardly from one foot to another. "My daughter loves him. If he can be saved... I'm just not sure. The other dog just attacked him for no reason." He looked at the old man expectantly, clearly hoping that he would volunteer to pay for the surgery.

The old man opened and shut his lips as if mumbling. "I need to talk to my wife." He looked back up at the vet tech. "So, if he has the surgery, he will be fine?"

"No, not necessarily," the woman hedged. "We just don't know."

The man nodded and mumbled again, "I need to talk to my wife."

Emily had never before witnessed a more awkward situation. She felt oddly embarrassed. This was a private matter that was on exhibition for both her and the man three seats down from her. By her few glances in his direction, he seemed to be having just as much luck with ignoring the scene as she was. Though his magazine stayed in position, Emily was sure he hadn't flipped the page once.

Neither of them should be seeing this. Emily knew it wasn't her business. And yet she couldn't look away. Even more, she longed to do *something*.

But the pain of helplessness in the center of her chest reminded her that there was absolutely nothing she could do. The best course of action was to just pretend that she wasn't listening. Compartmentalize things. This was just an interesting little tableau that really had nothing to do with her, right?

"Sparkles is your dog, correct?" the receptionist asked Emily. Emily startled. She hadn't even realized that the receptionist had retreated to the back of the clinic before returning with a bulldog in a pet carrier.

Emily stood quickly. "Yes, Sparkles is mine. I mean he's my parents' bulldog. But I'm the one picking him up."

The receptionist set the carrier down and returned to her computer behind the counter while Emily moved to the customer side.

"It looks like your mom pre-paid, so you're all set." Handing Emily a small plastic bag, she explained rather impatiently, "Sparkles' medication is in the bag, along with instructions. He's been neutered and had his soft palate surgically shortened. Everything went well, and he should recover fine and be able to breathe easier now. We already went over everything with your mom when she called. He's such a sweetheart. Aren't you, Sparkles?"

The receptionist bent down and jabbered more sugary-sweet words into the bulldog's carrier. It was rather amusing that the woman seemed to have an easier time talking with animals than she did with people.

As soon as the receptionist said her goodbyes and handed Emily her mother's receipt, Emily picked up the carrier and headed for the door. Sparkles wasn't a big bulldog, but he wasn't a light-weight either. Feeling the weight spread from her hand to her shoulder, she wanted to get him in the car quickly. She ducked her head and didn't make eye contact with the two men as she walked past.

Though her exchange had momentarily paused the scene, Emily knew it was far from over, and she really couldn't even imagine a result to hope for. While part of her wished the receptionist had tarried a little longer so she could see what the men decided, another part of her knew no result could be good, and she was anxious to leave the horrible situation behind.

And she almost did.

With the men three steps behind her, she suddenly stopped, looking at the door just two steps in front of her.

She remembered.

Her breathing rapid, she swallowed with difficulty. Then she deliberately set Sparkles back down and resolutely turned back to the two men.

"I'm sorry," she began before she lost her nerve. "I couldn't help but overhear your tough situation. Would you mind if I said a quick prayer for you?" Though her voice quivered, she spoke loud enough for the older man to hear and understand.

Both men blinked in surprise, but then the younger man shrugged and said, "Sure."

Emily immediately bowed her head and closed her eyes. "Dear, Lord. You already know the details of what happened. You also know that one dog is hurt, and they aren't sure he'll make it. It's a tough situation and a difficult choice, and I don't know the right answer. Please give both of these men wisdom to make the best decision. Give them compassion for the dog and for each other. Please help the dog not to suffer, and give the vet wisdom and skill to do what is needed. If it be in Your will, please let the dog live and recover, but also take care of these two men so that it is not a financial burden that they aren't able to pay. I know that's a lot to ask, but you are a loving Father. I know you can direct and take care of these two men and the dog. Please do what is best for all involved. In Jesus' name, Amen."

Emily opened her eyes. "I'm so sorry this happened to you," she said earnestly. Then she turned and picked up Sparkles in his carrier once again.

Though she tried to keep her gaze steady, she couldn't help but see the man sitting right by the door. She hadn't noticed anything other than his open magazine before. Up to this point, he'd been a silent observer like her. And it wasn't the fact that he was a nice-looking man in a suit that she noticed now. It was the look on his face. It was a look of shock mixed with awe, as if he'd just seen something he'd never seen before.

Unfortunately, there was nothing that indicated whether that sight was a good one or not.

Emily's gaze darted back to the door a micro-second after it detoured, but that one glance at that man left her feeling utterly humiliated and sure that she'd just managed to offend everyone. She reached for the door handle, already longing for the cold air to cool her flaming cheeks. The bells overhead announced her exit as she pulled the door open to escape.

"Thank you," a hoarse voice called, stopping her once again.

Emily turned back around, focusing on the three men and the two clinic employees now staring at her.

"Thank you," the old man repeated, nodding emphatically.

"Yes, thank you," the younger man echoed. "That was very thoughtful of you."

Emily shook her head. "Please don't thank me," she answered. Then she smiled and shrugged slightly. "I almost walked away."

A Cinderella Christmas

Chapter Two

WITH Sparkles tucked into the backseat, Emily crawled into the front, shut the car door, and sat for a few minutes just breathing.

She still didn't know if she'd done the right thing. Her prayer probably didn't make a difference. The men may have just been polite by saying thank you.

She *did* know that it had all been awkward and embarrassing.

Emily was a stranger who had pretty much been eavesdropping on their already tension-filled crisis, and then she'd inserted herself into business that wasn't hers.

But it was something she had to do. At that moment when the exit was two steps away, she'd flashed back to herself sitting on the curb after her accident. She remembered what it felt like for all of those people to walk by her as if they didn't see her tears. That's when she'd turned around.

She was helpless to do anything to fix the situation, so she'd appealed to the only One she knew who could do something. Yes, it was awkward, humiliating, and probably against all social and political norms, but she couldn't walk away without letting the two men know that she saw them. Maybe it didn't make a difference to them, but it made a difference to her. She hadn't walked away. She had tried to help in an impossible situation, and she had shared the feelings of her heart that she usually tried to quell in the name of social acceptability.

Thank you, Lord, she prayed. *I don't know if I did the right thing. I don't know if I managed to glorify You in any way, or if I just managed to make a laughingstock of both You and me. But I didn't walk away. Thank you for giving me the courage. Please continue to help me see what you see, and use me to help those who hurt.*

Opening her eyes, Emily turned the key in the ignition. Though she'd calmed down, the sound of her SUV's engine roaring to life made her heart jerk with anxiety of a different kind. She breathed in and out slowly, deliberately relaxing her death-grip on the wheel.

She'd made it here. She could make it back.

Forty-five minutes. It would take forty-five minutes to drive home to the small town of Crossroads. She could do it.

It had been six months since her accident. Common sense told her that, by this point, it shouldn't be so difficult to drive. But it was. She tried to pretend that the anxiety was improving. If ever she mentioned it to her parents, they voiced the idea that she should maybe get counseling.

Emily didn't want to do that. It was getting better. She knew it was. And she really didn't want to relive the accident for a therapist. She already did that on her own every time she made a left turn, or slept, or let her thoughts roam, or...

She was getting better. She was.

Lord, please keep me safe as I drive. And keep everyone safe from me.

With the heartfelt prayer that she now prayed every time she drove, Emily took one last deep breath and backed out.

As usual, her senses stayed on high alert as she pulled out onto the street. They may have even be keener because of the additional stress she'd encountered at the vet clinic. Her eyes moved constantly, picking up every detail of her surroundings, and a few details that weren't even there. Even a little flash of light on a mirror or a bird flitting through the sky made her jump.

She continued her deep breathing as she made it to the highway. She fought the anxiety as cars passed going the opposite direction. How easy it would be for one of them to drift over to her side. With just one mistake, one simple twist of the wheel, she could lose control, drift into oncoming traffic, and it would all be over...

You're fine. Keep it together, Emily. She exhaled slowly, flexing her tense fingers on the wheel.

Emily hadn't wanted to do the favor for her mom and pick up her parents' dog from the vet. The clinic that performed the special palette surgery on bulldogs was about thirty miles from their small town of Crossroads, and it was in Brighton Falls—the same city where she'd had her accident. It didn't help that she was also driving her same SUV. Though she was thankful her vehicle hadn't been totaled, the feelings of panicky deja vu felt overwhelming at times. So far, the whole experience just confirmed why she didn't often drive to Brighton Falls. In fact, she avoided it like a bad stomach flu. However, if she hadn't agreed to pick up the dog, she would have needed to tell her mom why, and that would bring up issues she was not willing to admit.

Since her mom was busy packing Christmas boxes at the church, Emily had reluctantly agreed to drive to Brighton Falls after she finished teaching for the day and pick up Sparkles the bulldog.

"It's a good thing you're sleeping, Sparkles," Emily said aloud, desperately trying to distract herself from her anxiety. "I don't know if I could take it if you started howling."

Speaking to a dog didn't seem strange to Emily. In fact, it felt so good that she continued to do so. "After I drop you off at Mom and Dad's, I need to get home. I have a lot of data to go through. The students had tests this week. I also have to prepare some of our Christmas projects. I need to do a bunch of cutting. I could just have the students do the cutting, but since they're first graders, that would likely take all day."

Emily sighed. "You, know, I was really hoping everything with the accident would be resolved by Christmas, but I just don't think that's going to happen."

Putting her foot on the brake, Emily slowed down. She signaled for a left turn and entered the turn lane. She bit her lip as a flood of anxiety hit her. Deliberately, she looked up at the light, even though she'd been watching it for the last minute on her approach. It was red. She stopped and waited, her mind drifting tirelessly to a different intersection six months ago.

It had all happened so fast. Funny thing how it was exactly like in a movie. The characters are driving along, chatting about something. It's life as usual. You catch a flash of movement in the passenger side door. Midsentence, the car is hit. Without warning.

It seemed like with something so life-altering, there should be some foreshadowing—some premonition of what is to come. It's the shock of the trauma that your mind can't cope with. Realistically, the other driver had every right to sue her, and the waiting and wondering kept the anxiety and nightmares still so fresh that the shock and trauma stayed her ever-present companions.

"Two years. The other driver has two years to file a suit against me," she told Sparkles. "It's been six months. With the way the lawyer talked, it is looking like it'll be closer to the full two years until I know anything for sure. And I just don't know if I can live like this for that long, Sparkles."

The light changed, and Emily's heart jerked painfully. It was one of those evil flashing yellow arrows. She waited, biting her lip painfully. She glanced up at her rearview mirror, wondering if anyone behind her would be too mad if she just sat here and waited for an actual green arrow.

But no, there were two cars behind her insistently blinking their left turn signals.

She waited while three cars passed going the other direction. Finally, there were no other vehicles in sight. Emily pulled forward slowly into the intersection.

A soft whine came from the backseat.

Emily's heart felt like it was on a pogo stick with each leap causing her entire body to jerk a little. Checking again, she turned the wheel and stepped on the gas.

She saw movement out of the corner of her eye and immediately flashed back to six months ago. She cringed, expecting at any second to feel the impact of another vehicle slamming into hers.

But it never came. Instead, the SUV smoothly completed the turn and continued on its way, exactly as thousands of other cars had done at that same intersection. Exactly as the cars behind Emily did.

To all observers, it was a normal day and a normal left turn. But for Emily, there was nothing exact or normal about it.

She shrugged it off and readjusted in her seat. One at a time, she reached each sweating hand down and wiped it on her leggings.

One mile later, she turned into her parents' driveway and shut off the engine.

"Well, we did that, Sparkles," Emily said brightly, paying no attention to her shaking hands.

With the relief of arriving, her brain suddenly relaxed enough to remember the poor dog she'd left at the vet's office. Pausing for a few seconds with her hand on the door handle, she breathed another quick prayer for the two men and the dog. She realized that, unfortunately, this was yet another thing that she was going to need to hand over to God. She was sure that even two years wouldn't make the difference for this one. She would likely never know what happened to that dog. And yet again, there was nothing she could do about it.

Grimacing, Emily stepped out into the cold air and opened the door to the backseat.

"Oh, thank you, Emily!" her mom greeted, rushing to Emily's side in a flurry of coat, hat, and flying scarf. "I just got home from church. I would have never made it to the clinic before it closed. How is my boy, Sparkles?"

"I think he's fine," Emily said. "He slept most of the way home. I just heard him stir a few minutes ago."

"You hurry inside where it's warm," her mom ordered. "I'll get Sparkles. It feels like snow out here!"

Emily shook her head and took the handle of Sparkles' carrier from her petite mother. "I'll carry him, Mom. You just show me where you want him."

Emily had taken after her father in height and was at least eight inches taller than her dainty mother. However, Kim Jansen's short stature was in no way indicative of her personality. The perky brunette looked younger than the years that had earned her wisdom she wasn't afraid to distribute.

Relenting, Kim Jansen hurriedly led the way inside the house. "Just set him right there," she instructed, pointing to a corner by the fireplace. "I'll get him out and settled on his bed. There by the fire is his favorite place."

Emily wearily sat back on the couch while her mom fussed over Sparkles. Just being home at her parents' house seemed to ease some of her anxiety. The Jansen living room looked like a photo shoot for a Martha Stewart magazine. Seeing the gorgeous Christmas tree with all the ornaments from her childhood standing glowing and majestic in the bay window in front of her eased even more tension. For a few brief breaths, she felt weak but wrapped in a warmth that drew her heavy eyelids down.

Finally getting the dog positioned on the colossal dog pillow, Kim turned back to Emily. "You just stay there and relax, sweetheart. I'll get dinner ready shortly, and we'll eat when your dad gets home."

"Oh, I can't stay, Mom," Emily said quickly, her eyes popping open. "I have a ton of work to do for school."

"Do you intend to eat tonight?" Kim asked flatly, putting her hands to her trim hips.

"Of course," Emily replied.

"Then stay and eat with us. I'll give you an extra pair of hands to get things done faster. Do you need things cut out? You know, cutting paper has been my specialty since I was in kindergarten."

Emily laughed. "Ok, Mom. I'll stay. Wait a minute, maybe I should ask what we're having first. If it's meatloaf, I can't stay. I have a plate of cardboard I'd rather eat at home."

"No meatloaf," Kim said with a smile. "Tacos. I'm making tacos."

"Then I'll stay," Emily consented.

However, had she known that her mother's inquisition was about to begin, not even tacos could have made her stay.

Chapter Three

KIM went to the kitchen to begin the meal preparations, while Emily retrieved a bag from her SUV and took a seat on a barstool at the counter. Spreading out her supplies, she drew a mitten template on some cardstock, cut it out, and then began tracing over fifty copies of the mitten on construction paper.

"Have you heard from the lawyer?" Kim wasted no time in flinging over her shoulder as she browned the ground beef at the stove.

"No, and I would prefer not to," Emily said grimly.

"Why is that?" Kim asked, openly surprised.

Emily sighed. "When I hired him, he said that he would try to resolve things before the two-year mark. The other driver has two years from the accident to file a claim against me. He tried. He sent a letter and called, but received no response. But his 'trying' cost me $1,500."

Emily winced, remembering how difficult it was to write that check that was over the amount of her monthly mortgage. "I really don't want him to try anymore, and I don't even want to call him to find out if there have been any results. The one time I tried to contact him, since I hadn't heard anything in two months, I was charged a fee for him to review the case, talk to me, and tell me that there were no new developments."

"That's ridiculous!" Kim protested, her spatula poised like a weapon in her displeasure.

Emily shrugged. "There isn't anything I can do about it. At this point, I just have to wait until I receive notice that I'm being sued or the case is resolved and closed."

Kim's lips pursed. "If the lawyer isn't going to do anything, why do you need him? I think you should just fire him."

Emily sighed, watching dejectedly as Kim drained and seasoned the meat. Her mom was never short on opinions, even if she didn't fully realize the details.

"I don't really have a choice, Mom," Emily finally said, placing the mittens she'd cut in a neat stack. My insurance advised me to get a lawyer. They sent me official notification that their maximum limit isn't anywhere close to the total cost of the other driver's medical bills. It's possible that, since I was found to be at fault for the accident, I may be held responsible for the difference in her bills. Realistically, they are right. It was my fault, and if I had the money, I would willingly pay to try to make things right. But I don't. Even so, it is a very real possibility that I will be sued for a large sum of money."

"Don't talk like that!" Kim reprimanded, jerking the spatula Emma's direction as if it was a gavel she was using to call the court to order. "People get in accidents all the time. That's what insurance is for."

Emily shook her head. "That's what everyone thinks. 'You don't have to worry if you have insurance. Accidents are what you have insurance for.' But that isn't true. Mom, I have a $50,000 limit on my insurance policy for the medical expenses for the other driver. That's it. I really wish my insurance agent had let me know years ago that 50K may not be enough. If he had advised me to raise it, I definitely would have. But none of that matters now. The last I knew, the other driver's medical expenses were over $150,000 and still counting."

Kim's mouth dropped and her hand grating the cheese paused with yellow shreds hanging from the other end like a clump of healthy grass in need of a mow. "That much? For a broken foot?"

"Mom, she pretty much shattered her foot," Emily said, reaching across the counter to take the cheese and grater from her mom and finish the process. "She's had multiple surgeries to try to piece it back together. She may still be in physical therapy and accruing expenses. I just don't know. That's one of the hardest parts. I hurt someone, and I have no idea how she is doing. All I can do is pray."

Kim grumbled as she opened a can of black olives with enough force to send olive juice splashing across the counter. "If she hadn't been driving such a dinky car, she wouldn't have gotten hurt."

Emily shook her head again, feeling like she was arguing a case she had no hope to win. Mom was determined to be her champion, no matter if it was rational or not. "It doesn't matter if she was driving a tricycle. I was at fault. If I hadn't failed to yield, she wouldn't have hit me."

"I'm sorry, sweetheart," Kim sighed, pushing the bowl of olives her direction, as if giving her permission to sneak a few out when she "wasn't looking."

"I know it's all very upsetting to you," Kim continued, "but I really think you're taking too much of the blame for yourself. You don't know how fast she was going. You don't know if she even tried to avoid the accident. You said there was no screech of brakes or marks on the pavement. You said she didn't swerve either."

"No," Emily admitted quietly, her mind immediately replaying the scene that always remained in the forefront of her mind. "There was just the impact. I tried to get away, but there was nowhere to go." She reached down and absently rubbed her hand where it still ached on occasion.

After the accident, the pain in her hand had gotten worse,

and she'd had it looked at by a doctor. While there had been no fracture, the soft tissue damage from wrenching the wheel had taken a long time to heal. But that fact made her only feel worse. As bad as her hand had hurt, she knew it was nothing compared to what the other driver must have felt.

Finally, picking up the scissors and red construction paper again, she continued. "All of that is irrelevant, Mom. The simple facts are that I failed to yield and caused an accident in which someone was hurt. I am the bad guy here. I am the one who broke the law. You tell a story of how an accident happened, and I'm on the wrong side. I'm the one everyone hates. What makes it even worse is knowing that it could have been worse. Mom, I could have killed someone! There could have been children in the other car!"

"But you didn't, and there weren't," Kim came around the counter and put a comforting hand to her shoulder as she perched on the barstool next to her. "Emily, even in this, God is merciful. Yes, it could have been worse, but it wasn't."

"But it still could be," Emily's voice trembled. "I still could be sued. I could lose everything, including my house, and have money garnished from my wages."

"Emily, it will be okay," Kim squeezed her shoulder gently and picked up another pair of scissors and an outlined mitten. "You're getting all worked up over 'what ifs.' There's so much you don't know. For instance, won't the other driver's insurance pay for what yours doesn't?"

Emily shrugged. "I have no idea. Maybe they'll pay for part, maybe they won't. It depends on her insurance and coverage."

"Sweetheart, you really need to think about this rationally." The tone of her voice was slightly reminiscent of when Emily was a child and overwrought about some mountain that resembled a molehill. "I don't think it at all likely that you'll be sued. It would hardly be worth it. You're a teacher. You don't have any money for her to sue you over."

"No, I don't have much money," Emily agreed quietly. 'But dad does."

Kim startled, and the scissors in her hand stalled.

Emily was sure she read fear in her mother's eyes.

"But it was your accident," Kim objected. "They can't sue your dad."

Emily swallowed, but even that didn't make the words come past her dry throat any less painfully. "Technically, you're right. However, when I bought my SUV eight years ago, Dad paid for part of it as my college graduation present, and he co-signed to get me a better interest rate. His name is on the vehicle that was wrecked. I specifically asked the lawyer if they could sue my dad, and he thought that a valid enough concern to research it. Several hundred dollars later, he informed me that would be an unlikely but not impossible scenario."

"Well, that's a relief." As if that solved the problem, Kim's scissors once again began whizzing around the mitten shape.

Knowing things weren't quite as clear-cut as her mom would like to believe, Emily continued. "Unfortunately, people don't actually behave in the most rational manner, and I suppose someone could sue someone else for any reason, rational or not. The lawyer said 'unlikely,' but that is nowhere near a 'no, it can't happen.' While I really doubt they would try to sue Dad directly, I think it far more likely that they would sue me for an exorbitant amount, counting on the possibility that Dad will come to my rescue and pay on my behalf for any settlement. After all, Dad is well-known and owns more property in both Crossroads and Brighton Falls than just about anyone else. It's no secret that I'm his daughter."

"But most of our assets aren't liquid," Kim protested. "They are in property and with your dad's company."

Emily shrugged. "That won't matter. Getting a judgment against Dad would be difficult. They would only get money from him if he voluntarily gave it to solve my problems."

Kim's lips pursed with concern, but her focus remained on her scissors. With her voice threaded with a false calm, she replied. "Honey, there is no sense worrying about it. You don't know that you'll be sued. From what you say, you won't know for another year and a half. You can't put your life on pause and spend all of your energy worrying about something that very well might not happen."

Emily put her scissors down and wearily rested her head in her hands. "I know, Mom."

She looked around, trying to draw comfort from the sight of the evergreen garland and twinkle lights twisting their way up the stairs, the pictures of her wonderful childhood lining the wall, and the sense of peace that usually accompanied being home.

But comfort was elusive, and she finally admitted. "I don't know how to not think about it. It's a huge cloud that follows me wherever I go and whatever I do. I feel like a bad person. Even though I didn't do it on purpose, I hurt someone. Badly. And I don't know how it's going to end. I could lose everything and be a financial burden to my family, all because I thought a stupid light was green."

Mom's hand rested comfortingly on Emily's back, and she reassured, "Emily, whatever happens, your dad and I will be right beside you. Your brother too. He's already said that he'll do whatever he can to help. We won't let you fall."

"But, mom!" Emily yelped, the hiccup of a sob escaping. "I don't want to drag everyone down with me. I won't allow Dad to bail me out. That's what they'd be gambling on. No. I'd pay what I could and then file for bankruptcy."

Kim's lips grew taut, and her eyes hardened. Emily knew she'd reached her mom's limit. She could only get so much compassion and understanding until Kim's tactics turned to tough love.

"Emily Jansen, has God abandoned you so far?" Kim asked flatly.

Not trusting her voice, Emily merely shook her head slightly.

Kim nodded firmly. "He has no intention of abandoning you today or tomorrow either."

"I know that, Mom," Emily replied softly. "But knowing that in my head and feeling it are two entirely different things."

"Sometimes you can't listen to your feelings," she said, accepting no excuse. She picked up the paper and returned to cutting. "Feelings lie. Right now, you're afraid. You're not taking a single step forward because you're scared that one mile down the road there might be a pothole. But you aren't there yet. There might not be a pothole." She turned and looked earnestly into her daughter's eyes. "Sweetheart, you can't pause your life because of what may or may not happen. You have to keep living."

Emily couldn't manage to respond. And really, it wouldn't do any good anyway. Mom wasn't telling her anything that she didn't already know. How many times a day did she give her worries over to the Lord? She knew there was nothing to be gained by worrying. She knew it was only harming herself, and that the only One who could do something was God. Yet, about two minutes after she left the problem in God's capable hands, she snatched it back again, endlessly thinking it through, trying to prepare herself for what may come and, yes, trying to punish herself for what had already happened.

But she couldn't tell that to her mom, mostly because she already agreed with everything Kim was saying. Mom was right. The problem was her. Knowing that only intensified the feelings of guilt. She had been stupid to get in an accident, and now she still couldn't stupidly manage to give it over to God and live trusting Him. All of it was her fault.

No, the best course of action was to nod in the right places and wait until her mother's lecture was over.

"You can't keep putting your life on hold." Kim continued solemnly, not seeming to realize that she was preaching to the choir. "You've never been a social butterfly, but I don't think you've been on a single date since the accident, nor have you even done anything fun with friends. It's all I can do to get you to come over here for dinner or a game night. Emily, it isn't healthy. I don't know if it's your way of punishing yourself, but it needs to stop. You need to give yourself permission to live again. What happens in a year and a half is going to happen regardless of what you do today. And whatever happens will be okay because God and your family will be right beside you."

Emily shut her eyes and shook her head. Her mom came closer to the truth than she was willing to admit. Emily was angry with herself. Very angry. If she hadn't been so stupid, she wouldn't have hurt someone and put herself and her family at risk. It was her fault, and she felt that every bit of that blame deservedly belonged solely on her shoulders.

"That's kind of the whole point, Mom," Emily finally managed. "Everyone knows you'll help me. That's the reason why I very well might get sued. I know you love me. I know you'd do anything for me. But I can't let you."

A stubborn light shone in Kim's eyes, and she opened her mouth to respond. However, Emily's dad stepped into the kitchen from the direction of the garage, immediately ending the discussion.

"How are my girls?" Peter Jansen asked brightly.

"Fine, Dad," Emily lied, pasting a smile on her face in relief. For now, her dad's presence marked the end of her mom's lecture and any conversation about the accident. Emily really didn't want to discuss the accident around her dad. If he knew that she'd already paid $1500 in lawyer fees, he would insist on paying it. If she refused, she would likely soon receive a refund check from her lawyer since her dad would go around her to pay the bill directly on her behalf. Her parents weren't rich in terms of cash, but she knew her dad would sell everything he owned if it meant helping her.

She couldn't let that happen. Hopefully, Mom would keep

quiet about the lawyer bill, or at least make Dad understand the importance of not helping her.

"Em, are you staying for dinner?" Peter asked hopefully, coming toward the two ladies.

"Yes, but I can't stay for games or anything afterward," Emily responded, not wanting him to get his hopes up. "It's a school night."

"We'll take what we can get," he said, planting a gentle kiss to her temple.

Emily stacked up her finished paper mittens and busily helped her mom with setting the table and putting the finishing touches on dinner. The next hour was a welcome relief. On the one hand, it felt strange that Emily was happiest when putting on a façade that she was fine. Her smiles were all fake. Her laughter was forced. Her conversation was deliberately cheerful. Yet pretending was the only time her mind wavered from its normal thought pattern. Being alone with her own thoughts was the worst feeling of all, and any escape from herself became a welcome distraction—one she desperately needed.

After dinner, Emily packed up her supplies and construction paper mittens back into her bag. She donned her coat, gave Sparkles a pet, and said her goodbyes. Ever the gentleman, her dad walked her to her car.

"It feels like there may be snow on the way," Emily said, shivering as she drew her hand out of her pocket to unlock the door.

"The weatherman seems to think it's coming," her dad answered. "I hope we'll get a nice, white Christmas, though I know you aren't fond of snow."

"I like to look at it just fine. I just don't like to drive in it."

Her dad opened the car door for her. "Just let me know anytime you need a lift, Em. I'll play your chauffer anytime."

Emily smiled and stood on her tiptoes to plant a kiss on his cheek. "Thanks, Dad."

She started to step into the SUV.

"Em?"

Her dad's voice stopped her, and she turned back.

"Whether you get sued or don't, it will all be okay."

Emily's breath sucked in painfully. Her dad understood more than he let on. He didn't need all the details like her mom. Instead, he observed and understood enough to realize the issues at hand, and then he dispensed bits of wisdom at the most unexpected times.

He sounded so confident as if there were no doubt in his mind that everything would be fine. Emily knew enough about her dad to realize this wasn't a confidence of ignorance. And she longed for a bit of that same assurance.

"How do you know, Dad?" Emily asked quietly. "There is no guarantee that I won't get sued and lose everything. Horrible things happen to Christians all the time, and God doesn't prevent them."

"I know because I know God," Peter said simply. "I don't know if there is sunshine or a storm up ahead. But I do know that if He allows something to happen, it's because He intends to carry you through it. Maybe it isn't even about you. He could have stopped your accident and didn't. He doesn't waste pain, Em. He has something good planned. Maybe it's something good for someone else. If that's the case, praise God! He's using you to do it."

"But it's scary," Emily said, feeling very much like a five-year-old wanting to remain safe and comforted in her daddy's arms. "I don't want to go through storms."

"I know, Em," Peter said, folding her into a hug. "But whatever comes, your family will be with you, and so will God."

It was something she had thought of before and wondered about in her many hours of obsessive thinking. God could have prevented her accident and didn't. He also could have prevented the multitude of worse things that had happened to other people, and He hadn't.

God could have made her look up at that light sooner. He could have sent the information to the right part of her brain sooner. After all, He was the God of the universe. If he'd wanted to, he could have made her car not start that morning or even picked the vehicle up and moved it out of the way.

And He hadn't.

On the other hand, He also could have allowed the other driver to be injured worse or killed. He could have let Emily face injury or death herself.

But He hadn't.

Wondering why would drive her crazier than she was already.

Maybe Dad was right. Maybe whatever God allowed to come her way had a purpose that He intended to use, both for her good and the good of others. Unfortunately, she may never know what any of that "good" consisted of, and faith of that variety felt completely lacking for Emily at the moment.

As she'd told her mom earlier, knowing something in your head and living that knowledge in your life were two entirely different things. Yet again, Emily felt up against an impossible task.

"Thanks, Dad," Emily said, planting another gentle kiss to her dad's cheek before finally slipping into the driver's seat. Trying to keep the sight from her dad, Emily wiped at the hot tears streaming down her cold cheeks and waved to him one last time as he walked back to the front door.

Now she was alone with herself once again.

She turned the key, and the engine roared to life, whisking away all of her father's comforting words like delicate snowflakes tossed by a fierce wind.

Emily shivered and turned the heat as high as it would go.

She flipped the headlights on.

Slow breath in. And out.

You can do it. It's just a ten-minute drive. You're okay.

But it was a lie. She still wasn't okay. She wouldn't be okay for at least 18 more months. If not forever.

Chapter Four

Grant

THE blue notebook on the table looked at Grant accusingly.

Grant tried to ignore it and continue stirring the spaghetti sauce, but he felt the accusation of its presence even when his back was turned. It felt like someone was watching him, only the someone was a notebook that belonged to someone else.

It was ridiculous. It wasn't like he'd stolen the notebook, but his conscience didn't seem to realize that his motives in taking it had been pure.

With the sauce bubbling nicely and the noodles in the pot, Grant walked back to the table and picked up the notebook once again. It was small, about a 5x7 size. Outwardly, there was nothing remarkable about the plain, spiral bound pad with a blue cover. Usually, such items could be purchased for around a dollar.

Finding the words that had first captured his attention,

Grant ran his fingers over them, as if words so profound should have texture to them—a sensation that could be felt physically as well as emotionally and spiritually.

Maybe his motives weren't entirely pure.

He wanted to meet the woman who had penned these words.

Grant grimaced. If only the receptionist at the vet clinic had been more helpful, then he could have returned the notebook, met the woman, and detoured his mind from its current obsession.

Truthfully, though, his fascination hadn't started with the poem, or even with the notebook. It had started the instant the woman had stopped and talked to the two men at the clinic. Even then, he may have been able to stick the whole experience in the "interesting" category and gotten over it.

However, after finally retrieving his cat, Grant had finished his business with the rather surly receptionist and turned to leave when his gaze had landed on the blue notebook sitting beneath one of the chairs by the door. He knew instantly that it belonged to her, but by now, she was long gone. Still, he hurried to retrieve it and take it back to the receptionist.

"This notebook belongs to the woman who was in here earlier. I think her dog was named Sparkles," he announced quickly.

The receptionist held her hand out distractedly. "I'll keep it back here in case she comes back for it."

Grant hesitated. "Can't you just call her and let her know that she left it here?"

The receptionist offered a tolerant smile that more resembled a grimace. "I don't know who she is. She was picking the dog up for someone else. Her mom, or her sister. Or maybe it was her friend. I don't know. It's not as if it were a wallet. I'll keep it, and if it's important, she'll be back for it."

The woman held her hand out expectantly.

Grant drew the notebook back protectively. A quick glance around the office revealed stacks of files mixed with an assortment of magazines and other mail on every surface around the computer and countertops. If he gave the notebook to the woman, it would be lost in the chaos of the office, forgotten, and eventually assigned to the trash.

"Maybe there is a name or address in here somewhere," he said, stalling as he opened the binding.

Grant got the impression that if he hadn't just handed over a large sum of money, the woman would have actually rolled her eyes.

"It's a notebook," she said. "Whoever owns it probably has a dozen more just like it."

To the casual observer, it really did look like it was just a scratch pad. Grant's eyes skimmed past to do lists and shopping lists that included the same grocery staples over and over, just labeled with different dates.

But in between the mundane lists, there seemed to be something else that was not nearly so ordinary. Poems, thoughts, ideas, and bits of wisdom interspersed like pretty seashells in a vast expanse of sand.

This was an everything book. Anything worth writing down went in this notebook. If the owner needed to remember to buy toilet paper, she took out her notebook and wrote it down. If she had an observation, heard a prayer request, was struck by a scripture, or had an inspiration, it went in the book. It contained anything and everything worth remembering and acted as a record of a life that was both mundane and exceptional. The information most people kept in a planner or on a cell phone, housed on these pages, and Grant found the precise cursive script to be a beautiful illustration of a beautiful soul.

Quickly, he turned the pages back to the front of the notebook, hoping that his gaze would land on a name or contact info. Instead, they fell on several lines all neatly left aligned, with words extending in various-length tails to the end of the line.

It was a poem. But it was more than that. It was a prayer. And even more than that. It was deeply personal.

> *Give me eyes to see what isn't shown,*
> *Ears to hear what isn't said,*
> *Hands to do what You want,*
> *And the courage to not walk away.*

Grant's heart wrenched in a strange way at the words. Looking above the poem, several more words scrawled randomly across the page. It was a pre-writing attempt, as if the writer were snatching random words from the air before they landed on the page in a coherent form. Turning the page, he found more lines neatly written. It wasn't another poem, but more like an exquisite thought painted on the page with the ambling strokes of a pen.

> *How many people do I pass every day and not even notice their tears? Sometimes I do notice that life is a struggle for someone, but it's not convenient or comfortable, and I hurry along on my busy day. But what if I could see what God sees? What if I could hear the silent prayers never voiced? Lord, let me see through your eyes—to see those who are asking for help without words. Let me hear their cries and notice when life is hard. Most of the time, I know I won't be able to fix it, but I can let them know someone cares. Show me the people sitting on the curb of my own path, and don't let my feet walk away.*

Grant glanced up at the receptionist and flashed her an endearing smile. "This notebook is important. I know you're busy, but if you give me the contact info, I can call the woman's mother and make sure this gets back to her."

Whereas most women seemed susceptible to Grant's tall, dark, and handsome looks, even his rakish grin and imploring brown eyes fell flat on a woman apparently immune to his charms.

The receptionist sniffed disdainfully, and Grant knew he had already spent any favor he may have earned previously. "I cannot give you the contact info for one of our patients. Now, if you'll please give me the notebook, I have other matters that need my attention." She pointedly held out her hand once again.

"Are you going to call about it?" Grant asked, holding the notebook's spiral binding firmly in his hand.

The receptionist sighed irritably. "Is there a name in the notebook?"

"No," Grant replied.

"Then we don't know for sure who it belongs to. There have been a lot of people in and out of the office today. I'm not going to waste my time trying to locate the owner of a notebook that probably isn't worth a dollar!"

Grant reached in his wallet and pulled out a card. "This is my number. Since the notebook is of such little value, it shouldn't be a problem to take it with me. If someone comes looking for it, please give them the number on that card to call. Meanwhile, I will try to find the owner myself so you won't need to be bothered with it."

"Suit yourself," the woman replied. While she accepted the card, she then dismissed him with a wave of her other hand.

"Dad!" a voice called.

At his daughter's call and the sound of the front door shutting, the words on the lined page came back into focus, and

Grant's memories of earlier shifted to the background of his mind.

"I'm in the kitchen, Mila!" Grant called. But instead of moving to greet his 14-year-old daughter, he stood there, still transfixed by the words in the notebook.

"Hi, Dad!" Mila said, cheerfully entering the room. "What are you looking at?"

"Just a poem in a notebook I found." He closed the pages gently and set it on the counter. "How was basketball practice? Are you ready for some spaghetti?"

"Sure," she said, taking a perch on one of the barstools at the counter. "Practice was fine. Jessica's mom said she'd be happy to give me a ride home tomorrow after practice if we needed."

Grant nodded. "I'll text her. I should be able to pick you up tomorrow, but practices next week might be difficult with my schedule. If she's willing to give you a ride, that may help me get more work done before you get home."

Grant soon had two plates of spaghetti on the table. After saying grace, they began eating.

Mila kept a running monologue about her day, which mostly consisted of a report on who said what. Grant tried to nod in the right places, but he was so distracted that his daughter's words were just sounds instead of conveying actual meaning.

Mila's chatter gradually dwindled, and Grant didn't notice. As if on autopilot, he finished his spaghetti and carried it to the sink. The sounds of running water and the clink of dishes were the only sounds in the room, but Grant's thoughts rang loud enough to drown out any sound, or lack thereof. Finishing loading the dishes into the dishwasher, he dried his hands on a towel and turned around, intending to collect his things and head into his home office to get some work done.

But the sight of his daughter still at the table, pushing

around a half-eaten plate of spaghetti with a fork, gave him pause. He hadn't even realized she was still in the room.

"Aren't you hungry, Mila?" he asked, working to put away the last of the dinner supplies.

"Not really," Mila answered, pushing her chair back and standing to carry her plate to the sink.

Feeling slightly unsettled, Grant watched her face. He felt a brief inkling that something really was wrong, but he quickly dismissed it. If she wanted to talk, she'd talk.

He quickly finished wiping off the counter and grabbed the notebook and his phone.

"I'll be in my office," he announced. "I have some work to get done."

He glanced down at his phone to check his messages as he headed out of the kitchen.

Then, suddenly, he stopped.

Slowly, he turned back around and looked once again at his daughter's face. She'd cleaned off the table with a rag and was now taking a textbook out from the backpack at her feet.

What if there really was something wrong? What if that dull light in her eyes and the sad turn or her mouth wasn't just because she had homework to do? His mind raced back over what she'd said about her day, but he couldn't recall anything, either good or bad. He hadn't been paying attention, and the space in his mind where there should be information remained completely blank.

It wasn't unusual that Grant didn't know exactly how to deal with his daughter. When she was little, all he had to do was wrap his arms around her and pull her into his lap when she was upset. But that didn't seem to work as well since she was older. Playing and running around with her outside, or turning the living room into a huge blanket fort, also seemed to be losing its thrill. He didn't know how to interact with her anymore. He couldn't read her thoughts and emotions.

Fortunately, Mila was a good girl with a sweet personality, which was a great blessing. He knew he didn't always give her his full attention because he always assumed that she was fine.

And again came the question. What if she wasn't fine?

Grant gripped the notebook in his hand tightly, keenly feeling the weight of its contents.

His phone beeped as a text came through.

> SUSAN—3:00 MEETING TOMORROW AFTERNOON. NEED TO SEE WHAT U HAVE 4 STORY.

Nothing. The short answer for his nagging boss was that he had nothing he could submit for the newspaper's latest edition.

He shut his eyes, feeling the stress of the moment wash over him. He needed to get some work done.

Feeling pain in his hand, he looked down to see the spiral binding of the notebook leaving a tattooed imprint on his palm.

His jaw tensed. He couldn't do it.

Grant's feet took him back to the table. He pulled out a chair and sat down beside Mila.

Chapter Five

MILA looked up at her dad in surprise.

Grant swallowed with difficulty and captured his daughter's gaze with his own. "I'm sorry, Mila. I don't think I did a good job of listening when you were talking about your day during dinner. I feel like you might be upset about something, but I have no idea what. Could you please tell me again about your day? This time I promise I'll listen."

Mila blinked and then shrugged. "There isn't much to tell." Then she stopped and rummaged through a bunch of loose papers as if looking for something.

Grant waited.

The truth was that his daughter downright scared Grant. In the instances where she got too emotional for him to ignore, he normally retreated to his office where he'd make a call to his mom. Grandma would show up promptly, catch Mila's tears, and make things all better in a relatively short time period. When it was safe, Grant would emerge from his office to the aroma of freshly baking chocolate chip cookies and the smiling faces of his mom and daughter.

Even now, just the thought that she might be upset made

him long for his office and escape, but he knew it was too late in the day for an SOS call to his mom. She wouldn't be able to come out on a rescue mission.

"Everyone is talking about this stupid dance," Mila finally flung out irritably, tossing to the table a flyer about a "Christmas Wonderland" school dance.

Grant realized she'd mentioned the dance before. If he'd paid attention then, he would have realized that the mention of it was what had drained her previously happy mood. And now, mentioning it a second time seemed to bring her close to tears.

"Why is the dance stupid?" Grant asked, nervously running a hand through his already tousled hair. He was in over his head. He had no idea why a dance would be "stupid" to a 14-year-old, nor did he have a clue why a "stupid dance" would be upsetting.

Oh, how he needed Kristi! It was the same thought that scurried through his mind about a hundred times a day. Though it had been a full five years, his longing and need for his wife never seemed to ease. If only Kristi were here… She would know exactly what to say to Mila. She could read and understand what their daughter was thinking and feeling, and like magic, she could make it better, just like she always did.

As Grant well-knew, all the longing a heart could feel still couldn't manage to bring a loved one back from the dead.

Kristi would surely know why a dance was stupid, without even asking. Instead, he was left to ask what was probably a very stupid question about what was probably quite obviously a "stupid dance."

"Everybody is talking about it," Mila said, leaning back in her chair and folding her arms around her front grumpily. "They're gossiping about who is going with whom or who is going to ask who. That's all anyone is talking about." She paused for a breath, then added hurriedly. "I already know you won't let me go. I don't even want to go. Everyone is just being so stupid about it. I'd rather wait until high school to go to a dance, like you said."

Grant started to ask another question, then stopped. He started again, but then stopped again. He was lost. If the dance was stupid and she didn't want to go, then why was she upset? But, he was terrified that if he asked that question, she'd get even more upset that he was so insensitive!

Grant's phone beeped again. His gaze swerved down of its own volition.

> SUSAN: U NEED TO GIVE ME SOMETHING, GRANT. I'VE BEEN PATIENT, BUT OTHERS AREN'T SO MUCH. I NEED TO SHOW THEM MORE THAN COVERAGE OF THE COUNTY FAIR.

Grant swallowed with difficulty, Susan's words sending a stab of alarm straight through him. Very deliberately, he flipped the phone to silent and turned the screen face down on the table.

Then he turned back to his daughter, still at a loss as to what to say.

Fortunately, Mila needed very little urging other than a willing set of ears. After her gaze drifted up as if checking to see that her dad's focus really was still on her, she continued, this time a little more shyly with her voice soft. "I guess it just got me thinking that eventually, I'd like to go to a dance. I'd like to get a new dress and fix my hair like in a magazine. But I won't have Mom to help me. How am I supposed to know what looks good? Who will help me with my hair and makeup? She won't be here for any of that. Not for my dances... my graduation... my wedding. She won't. And I need her!" The last part ended in a sob that was quickly muffled as Grant pulled his daughter into his arms.

Grant brushed her hair back with his hand and soothed her with soft shushing sounds, even as his own eyes filled with tears. "Mila, it's going to be okay. I know it's not the same, but we'll figure it out. Maybe Grandma can help you with that stuff."

Mila pulled back into her own chair as a sound that seemed hallway between a cry and a giggle bubbled out up past her lips. "Dad, I love Grandma, but I'd really rather not have her fashion advice. I don't want to look like a teen from forty years ago!"

Grant smiled. "We have other family and friends who would love to help you, Mila. But I'm not really worried about it. Your mom isn't here, but she left you with a whole lot of beauty, intelligence, and great fashion sense. You're going to do fine on all of the outward stuff. What's going on inside is what I want to make sure is okay. You're worrying about things way far in the future, but what I really think is that you're missing your mom today."

Mila's eyes filled with tears once more. "I really am, Dad. I miss her so much. I like being with my friends. I like hearing them talk. But sometimes all I can think about is how they still have their moms, and I don't. Then I think about everything in the future and how nothing is going to change. It's not like I'll ever get my mom back, at least not here on earth."

"Sometimes, you have to take one day at a time, or you'll drive yourself crazy." Grant spoke from experience. It seemed almost hypocritical for him to give such advice when many days were still a struggle to get up in the morning, let alone making it through an entire 24 hours.

Nevertheless, he continued, giving his daughter advice that he should be taking himself. "Let God get you through today, and when you get to tomorrow, let Him get you through that one, too. Mila, I promise you that we'll make it work. I don't know how, but God will help you through, and I will be right beside you. I will make sure you have someone to help you with all that stuff. I'll even offer my own opinion if you want it. I'll take lousy pictures and threaten any boy who dares to take you on a date. Don't worry, Mila. I plan on sitting in the front row and thoroughly embarrassing you with my loud cheering at every life event in all of your tomorrows."

A hesitant smile whisked past the corners of her mouth. "Thanks, Dad. I know I'm being silly, and I shouldn't worry about it. I guess I'm just tired, and I've been thinking about Mom a lot."

Grant sighed, feeling like he was really screwing things up. "Mila, I don't think you're being silly. That's not what I meant. Thinking about all of those things is natural. I think about them too. It's good to grieve, and part of that is feeling sad at all the things that could've been. But you can't stay there. Your mom passed away, and you won't get to have all of those special moments with her like other girls do. It's not fair, and it's never going to be fair. But it will be okay, and we will find a way to help you enjoy everything that life has for you, one day at a time."

Mila nodded and then threw her arms around Grant. "You always make me feel better, Daddy. Thank you."

Grant's heart melted. He wrapped his arms around his daughter and longed to freeze time.

Hearing his phone vibrate against the table with another text message, he had the sudden urge to throw the thing across the room.

The slight interruption broke the moment. Mila pulled out of his arms and sat back in her chair, staring gloomily at the textbooks in front of her. "I guess I'd better get my homework done. Tomorrow comes awfully fast."

"I need to get my work done as well," Grant said with a grimace.

Still, he hesitated to retrieve his phone and get up. Though Mila seemed fine now and her face was clear from the earlier turmoil, he didn't want to leave her alone. He wanted to be with her.

"Why don't I go get my laptop and work out here with

you?" he asked with sudden inspiration. "Maybe if we're together, the work won't seem so lonely and boring."

Mila nodded eagerly. "And if we finish really quick, can we pop popcorn and watch a movie?"

Grant laughed. "Nice try, but it's a school night. I do have some cookies that Grandma brought over. Maybe we can have cookies and milk when we are done."

"Deal!" Mila said brightly, hurriedly pulling out her papers and finding the correct place in her book.

Grant stood up and started to walk to his office to retrieve his laptop.

"Dad?" Mila's voice called hesitantly.

Grant turned once again.

"Dad, thank you for talking to me. I know you have a lot of work to do. You were headed to your office. And I heard your phone beep with texts. What made you stop to talk to me?"

More than her words, Grant heard what she didn't say: *You usually don't stop.*

Grant was quiet, waiting for the wave of guilt to subside. "I almost didn't stop, sweetheart," he finally replied. "But I read a poem tonight that made me think about all of the times we miss those who need help. I guess I'm just trying to listen better for when God tells me to stop walking."

Mila's gaze was curious. "Can I see the poem?

Grant nodded. Though he was slightly hesitant about sharing something that he really didn't have any business reading himself, he told himself that the person who wrote those beautiful words wouldn't mind them being shared. If anything, they were *meant* to be shared.

Finding the page, Grant handed the notebook to Mila.

She read silently, turned a few pages, and read some more.

Just when Grant feared she would never give it back, Mila

lifted her head. Tears ran in glistening streams down her face.

"Mila, what's wrong?" Grant cried, hurrying to put his arm around her shoulders.

Mila sniffled. "It reminds me about when Mom died."

"What do you mean?"

Mila shrugged. "A lot of people said they were sorry. We had people bring us food. But I remember when I went back to school, nobody seemed to know what to say to me. Most just ignored me. I know it wasn't on purpose, but I really wished that someone saw what I was feeling and at least said something—anything. But most people don't notice when others need a little help."

"You're right. I really don't think it's intentional, but we are so busy we just don't see, or we don't want to."

"I know it's been five years," Mila sniffled. "I probably shouldn't still feel so bad, but some days I do. A few weeks ago, I was crying in the locker room after practice. Nobody noticed. If they did, they didn't say anything. Maybe they just thought I had a rough practice and would get over it. Maybe they were busy trying to get their own stuff done. I didn't say anything, so they had no way of knowing what was upsetting me. But I do wish someone had asked."

Grant nodded. "I know I've been bad about not noticing when others need help. My own life has seemed so overwhelming that my eyes haven't been able to see what is outside of about a foot in front of me. The words in that notebook made me think. I want to pay better attention to when God would have my feet stop walking. That's why I stopped tonight and didn't go to my office."

"Thank you for stopping, Dad," Mila said, wrapping her arms around him in a hug once again. "I think I need to do better, too. I see people and wonder if maybe I should say something or do something. Then I worry that they'll get upset or think I'm stupid. But worrying about being embarrassed is a pretty silly reason for not doing something God would have me do. People are always talking about how they want God to speak to them. What if God is speaking, just not about the things we are expecting? What if He's speaking to us all the time, but we're ignoring Him?"

"That's a deep and scary thought," Grant replied, impressed by his daughter's thought process. "Unfortunately for me, I think you're right. I think of those times I had a little inkling that you were upset, and I talked myself out of stopping, instead heading to my office instead. Now I really do believe that was God urging me, and I didn't listen."

"But you did tonight."

Grant shook his head, not accepting the comfort. "So, I got it right once. All the times I got it wrong far outweigh that one little point."

Mila shrugged. "But that one little point made a difference for me. And this did as well." Mila handed the notebook back to Grant. "Where did you get it? Whose notebook is it?"

Grant told her about the vet's office, and the woman who had prayed with the two men then refused thanks, saying she'd almost walked away. Then he told her about how she'd left the notebook, and he'd taken it with him. "Now I realize what she meant by saying she'd almost walked away. She was referring to the words in this notebook."

"Wow," Mila said, thoroughly enthralled by his story. "She sounds like an amazing woman. Even if you hadn't told me that story, I'd still like to meet the woman who wrote that. Now I want to even more."

Mila hit on the one thought that had so obsessed him this evening.

"So would I," he admitted. "Apparently, I owe her a big thank you."

Mila's face clouded with confusion. "I thought you said you did meet her—at the vet's office."

"I saw her, but I didn't meet her. I told you how she prayed with those two men and left, but I never actually spoke to her."

"So, do you like her?" Mila asked, a mischievous smile playing about her lips.

Grant answered calmly, refusing to be baited. "I like her as much as you could like someone when you don't know her name or anything about her."

"Is she pretty?" Mila persisted, wiggling her eyebrows.

"Yes. Quite." Grant managed to maintain his stoic composure, but barely. He picked up his phone from the table and once again turned to retrieve his things from his office.

"So, you know more than one thing," Mila said, refusing to take the hint and let the subject drop. "You know she loves God. She's a thinker. She's compassionate. She's a writer. And she's beautiful."

Wordlessly, Grant sent Mila a wink and headed to the door.

"Are you going to?" Mila asked to his back.

"Going to what?" Grant flung back, hoping that playing dumb would earn him enough time to make it safely through the door.

"Try to find her?" Mila asked simply.

Grant stopped and turned to look at Mila with a smile, and he couldn't ignore her. At the sight of her relaxed but eager face, a firm resolve came over him. Feeling guilty over taking the notebook wasn't going to accomplish anything. There were much more important tasks that needed to be done.

Mila was right. He knew more than he'd realized about the woman who had penned those words. And it was just enough to dream.

"Yes," he replied with determination. "I don't know how, but I'm going to find her."

Chapter Six

THE squeak of a chair announced Grant's time had come. Oh, how he hated Susan's squeaky chair!

Sure enough, she stuck her head around the partition and called, "If you're ready, Grant, we'll meet in my office."

Grant used the excuse of gathering his papers to cover his smirk. Calling Susan's cubicle an "office" was like referring to an aquarium as a lake. But that was the way Susan was. She was professional and formal to the point of being ridiculous.

Grant walked across the aisle of cubicles to Susan's and took a seat in front of her desk.

He'd been dreading this meeting and rather wished his boss did have an actual office. The fact that their conversation could be heard by listening ears in the surrounding office space made his discomfort even more pronounced.

To her credit, Susan's cubicle really did have the rather formal look of an office. An impressive set of awards and degrees hung on the wall behind her desk. A stark abstract painting hung beside those. All books or papers maintained positions at their assigned posts, and Grant guessed that even the one, spiky plant dared not reach a single leaf to the wrong angle.

The only item that didn't fit into the category of austere was a small, wiry Christmas tree sitting atop her file cabinet. And from the second Grant entered the space, that little, out-of-place tree was what snagged his curiosity.

"What do you have for me?" Susan demanded, wasting no time on pleasantries.

Even as Grant handed Susan the manila file with his completed stories, he knew this wasn't going to go well.

Susan perused the folder, the flipping of papers and Susan's deepened scowl drawing taut Grant's already stressed nerves.

Grant's gaze flicked from Susan's terse expression to the brightly blinking lights on the little tree, wondering why his Scrooge of a boss would have such a decoration, especially when it was rather gaudily decorated. The blinking lights were too big, as was the haphazardly donned popcorn garland and the ornaments that looked constructed of colored paper.

The whole arrangement was definitely not a decorative piece Grant expected to find in the office of a chief editor at a rapidly expanding newspaper. In an age when most newspapers were swept aside with the wave of technology, The Brighton Daily was making itself relevant. Though Susan Martinez didn't carry sole responsibility for their success, she was definitely a contributor. There were many other execs in the company who innovatively played their roles, but Susan was in charge of content for many of their divisions. Having a cubicle as opposed to a fancy office was one of the ways she succeeded. She literally had her foot by the desk of every reporter she had, and she preferred to keep it that way.

Her son. Grant finally decided. The tree must have been decorated by a child, and Grant guessed that Susan's little boy was the designer.

With the mystery solved, he had little else to distract himself from the storm that seemed to be gathering on Susan's face.

"I believe those are all the stories I was assigned," Her objections were clearly about to erupt, and he would rather preemptively ward off such an event.

Susan closed the file and tossed it to her desk, her chair letting out a squeak of emphasis. "Yes, those were your assignments, which you completed adequately. But you have nothing more?" She tapped the cap of her pen impatiently on her desk and raised a dark eyebrow Grant's direction.

Susan wouldn't back down, even a little. Realistically, Grant should count it a miracle that his no-nonsense boss had been patient this long.

Being so focused on her career, Susan Martinez hadn't married until she was over forty. Now she had a son who Grant thought was about 8 years old. But, other than a rather gaudy and adorable little Christmas tree, motherhood hadn't softened Susan in the workplace at all. Every inch of her, from her high heels, to her perfectly manicured nails, to her dark hair, expertly highlighted and cut in a short, smart style, evidenced her competence and professionalism. Though she was older than Grant by more than ten years, she was an attractive woman, which, when combined with her dictatorial and driven personality, made her all the more intimidating.

Grant blinked. "I wasn't aware that I was obligated to complete more than those assigned to me," he said, certain that his best course of action was to pretend he had no idea to what she was referring. He was tired of these veiled expectations. If she was displeased with his work or was expecting something else, he wanted her to spell it out for him.

Susan scoffed. "Come on, Grant. Don't give me that. You're an award-winning journalist—at least you were five years ago. The Brighton Daily originally hired you with those qualifications, and before your wife passed away, you wrote some amazing stories that really put us on the map. We've tried to be understanding. When you said you wanted to stay local and scale back your assignments, we willingly obliged. But it's been five years. The understanding was always that eventually you would get back in the saddle and produce something of your former quality."

Grant pointed to the folder laying haphazard on her desk. "I believe there are some very nice human-interest stories already in my assignments. Have readers been complaining about my work?"

Susan's chair protested noisily with her shifting in her seat as if suddenly uncomfortable. "Of course not. Everyone loves your work. That is everyone who reads it, which right now includes the residents of our local area. We need more. Grant, you know we've already had good success with becoming a national media force online. But none of your articles are on subjects great enough to go viral. We put them online, and those who read them appreciate the stories, but they aren't nationally relevant and aren't something readers feel strongly enough to press the share button. My bosses want more, Advertisers want more. Grant, your position and salary aren't those of an inexperienced journalist, but your assignments are what we give our local recruits."

"But your local recruits don't write the stories the way I do," Grant protested. "You've told me before that our readership has steadily increased, as has my popularity. You're always trying to get me to take a higher profile in the community because of it."

"Yes, which you are unwilling to do," Susan snapped back.

At which point, Grant immediately regretted the direction of his argument. Really not wanting a lecture on two fronts, he tried to explain. "If people knew Grant Dillon was coming to their event, they would act differently, and I wouldn't get the same story as an anonymous someone in the crowd."

"That shouldn't even matter with the stories you cover," Susan shot back smartly. "Tell me, does it really matter if the sheep at the county fair know you're Grant Dillan?

Grant's lips tensed, and he closed his eyes briefly, his frustration evident. "I don't know what that you want, Susan. I complete every assignment given to me, and I do it well. It's not like I'm purposely not writing the big stories. If you want something different, assign me something different. No, I still don't want to be on the national correspondence team, and I'm not crazy about the idea of travel or the lengthy exposé-type story you seem to be wanting. I'm sorry, I can't just produce a Pulitzer prize-winning story because you want me to. Tell me what you want, and I'll do it. But don't toss me some vague dissatisfaction that my stories aren't going nationally viral. Sounds like a problem with advertising, not content."

Susan sighed and leaned back in her chair, which added its own whine of sorrow. "Grant, you have so much talent in your pen that you could make people cry with a story about a dirty candy wrapper. That's what we need. But we need it for a wider audience. The local people care, but we need a story that will touch the world. What I want is a Grant Dillon story that will make the world care."

Grant shook his head. "You aren't asking for much, are you?" he asked sarcastically. "You should know that a journalist never sets out to write something like that; it just happens."

"And with your talent, it should have happened by now for you," Susan bit back. Then, after a few more thought-filled squeaks from her chair, she continued "My bosses would write me up for saying this, but are you sure this is the right place for you? Maybe you need a change. Maybe you need to get on with your life and go where memories of Kristi won't haunt you. I've always thought you should be on TV, not just writing the words, but delivering them. You are charismatic. People like you. They trust you."

Grant stubbornly shook his head and fixed his gaze on the tree once more, as if wishing the soft-hearted woman who had let her son decorate a Christmas tree for her office would make a brief appearance. But instead, she seemed determined to push

Grant's every button.

Susan sighed and shrugged in exasperation. "I'll be honest, Grant. You've lost your fire, and I don't know that it will ever come back, at least not here for *The Brighton Daily*. After five years, I'm wondering if you are even capable of making the world care."

Through the fog of anger and encroaching despair, Susan's words suddenly penetrated to his consciousness. *A story that will make the world care.*

Grant sat up straight, and his eyes flew open wide. "I'll be right back," he said before dashing back to his desk. Almost frantically, he rummaged through his briefcase and pulled out the blue notebook and a page he had written last night when he should have been working on the stories for work.

Without sparing a glance any other direction, he hurried back to Susan's cubicle and immediately launched into telling the story of what had happened yesterday at the vet's office. Finally, he handed her the page he'd written. It really wasn't worth the scrutiny of another pair of eyes. It was just an outline of yesterday's thoughts and experience put to paper.

Once again, Grant waited as Susan read. He resisted the urge to drum his fingers on the corner of her desk and instead nervously bounced his knee up and down to the rhythm of the flashing lights on the Christmas tree.

Susan's gaze flickered up from the page, and she looked at Grant without saying a word.

"I know it's not a hard-hitting exposé, and I'm sure it's not at all what you had in mind," Grant rushed to explain. "It's still local, but couldn't it still be nationally relevant, or even worldly relevant? That paper is really just a rough outline, but it would basically be divided into two sections to show the contrast, but tied together by the story itself."

Susan raised her eyebrows, looking at him completely serious. "Grant, it's brilliant. You have to find this girl."

Grant winced. "I tried and will continue trying, but the vet's office was adamant that they wouldn't give me a single name. Even if I don't find her, I can do interviews and base it on my own experience."

Susan shook her head. "It won't work, Grant. If you don't have her and her story, then the entire article falls apart. We have to know what inspired her thoughts and made her write the poem in the first place. It's the difference between a primary and a secondary source. You *need* to have her."

"I'll call the vet again," Grant said wearily, not looking forward to another round with the surly receptionist.

Susan gave an overly dramatic sigh that elicited an even more obnoxious sigh from her chair. "For Pete's sake, Grant, it shouldn't be that difficult. Just pack on that charismatic charm and tell her you're Grant Dillon."

Grant retrieved the notebook and his paper and stood to leave, not a hint of amusement showing on his face.

"Grant," Susan called before he made it to the cubicle opening.

Grant turned.

"You know this is it, right? This is your story. And it is big enough that it will make your career and put *The Brighton Daily* on every media outlet there is. You write the story, and I will call in every favor and do whatever needs done to put it in every newspaper and network in the country. But we need it fast. Christmas is what will help sell it. We need it ready to go by Monday. That will give us a week for it to go viral before Christmas."

"That gives me less than a week to find her and write a story that changes the world," Grant ventured, his hesitation evident.

"Yes, it does. And you'd better take that deadline and get out of here before I change my mind," Susan said, turning to the calendar on her desk with a pen in hand. "Christmas is two weeks away. I really want that story tomorrow."

"No pressure," Grant quipped sarcastically.

"No. Tons of pressure," she retorted, equally serious. "It's make-or-break time, Grant."

And the meaning of that casually tossed cliché is what hung in the air the longest. If he delivered on the story, everything would be golden, but if he didn't…

Unfortunately, he understood the message very clearly. "I guess I need to go find a girl."

With one last glance at the blinking Christmas tree lights that now seemed to be a timer counting down the seconds, Grant left Susan's "office."

Back at his desk, Grant looked up the number for the vet clinic.

Lord, help me find her! He prayed desperately.

Now, not only was his heart depending on him finding the mysterious Cinderella, his job was, too.

Chapter Seven

GRANT shut the trunk of his car with a little extra force and turned to push his shopping cart to its parking lot cage.

Less than three hours into his new assignment, and he was already at a dead end. He had called Vets and Pets Specialty Hospital only to talk to the same lovely employee from yesterday. Once again, she had been less than helpful. Even after dropping his name, the woman refused to give him any information about the bulldog's owner.

After much cajoling, she had finally agreed to at least speak with her boss, the head veterinarian. She said she would explain the situation and ask his permission to pass along the information. But she warned that the vet was "by the book," and it was very unlikely that he would reveal personal information of a patient or seek to get involved in any way. More problematic at the moment was that the vet was on vacation until next week—at which time the receptionist assured Grant she would add it to the long list of other matters requiring his attention.

At that point, it wouldn't matter. Next week would be too late.

Grant had gotten off the phone with a headache and then proceeded to run down every lead he could think of—even trying to find information on people who owned French Bulldogs in the area. All to no avail.

Having achieved nothing except exhausting every last lead in the last two hours, Grant finally gathered his things, gently deposited the notebook into his briefcase, and left the office. He needed to stop by the store before picking Mila up from basketball practice.

Now, after grabbing a bunch of groceries he hoped he could throw together for dinner, he finished up by pushing the protesting cart so it could join its friends in the caged lineup. But his thoughts still weren't on his surroundings. In fact, he probably couldn't even report a single thing he'd just bought.

That notebook is the key, he thought amidst his mind endlessly mulling the problem over. That and its contents were really the only clues he had. Maybe instead of trying to find the woman at the vet's office, he should approach it as if he were trying to find the writer of the notebook.

He hadn't actually gone through every page of the spiral bound tablet. After his discussion with Mila last night, he hadn't been able to focus on his actual assignments. Instead, he'd spent the time writing his thoughts on the paper he'd showed Susan. By the time he'd finished, he'd said good night to Mila and been so very tired, he'd called it a good night for himself.

He'd paid for it this morning. After dropping Mila off at school, he'd spent every minute until his meeting with Susan working on the stories he should have worked on last night. In the end, all that work hadn't mattered. She had turned her nose up at his stories. With only one way to salvage the situation, and possibly his job, he now had to deliver on a story and a task that might very well be impossible.

If that notebook didn't contain a clue, like the writer's address randomly written on a page in the middle of the tablet, then he was completely lost.

Grant walked back to his car. Glancing at his watch, he saw that he still had about twenty minutes before he needed to pick up Mila. With the winter night descending so early, the darkness always made it feel so much later than the actual time on the clock.

Realizing how cold it was, his steps quickened. Right before reaching his car, he saw the bright taillights of a car backing out a few spots down from his. Out of the corner of his eye, he caught the flash of another light. Turning slightly, he saw the taillights of another car backing out from the row opposite.

They were directly across from each other and their tires would soon by vying for the same territory.

Surely they will see each other, Grant thought, expecting brake lights to flash from one or both vehicles. But they didn't. Instead, the lights announcing reverse still proudly displayed as the cars inched closer to each other.

"Watch out!" Grant yelled, waving his arms and running toward the vehicles. But it was too late. With a sickening crunch, the cars backed into each other, the impact finally triggering the brake lights on both cars. Doors slammed on the vehicles before Grant closed the distance.

Then the yelling started.

"What were you doing?"

"What was I doing? Are you blind?"

"This is a new car. You're going to have to pay for the damage!"

"Why would I pay for something that is obviously your fault!"

The dialogue went downhill from there. Soon, both the woman driver from the one car, and the man driver from the other car were yelling profanities at each other. Neither one of them had grabbed a coat, but the cold air didn't seem to bother them or tone down their hot anger. The man was tall and slim. He wore a baseball cap and was dressed in workout clothes. The woman was short, heavy-set, and clad in a pair of leggings and high-heeled boots. Her shirt was a busy animal print that seemed to have sparkles of some kind that kept flashing with the glow from the lights above the parking lot.

"Excuse me!" Grant said loudly, trying to get their attention.

Besides a few people gawking as they slowly walked by to and from the story, Grant remained the only person who ventured close to the arguing duo.

"Hey! Listen up!" Grant tried again, shouting this time.

When both pairs of eyes briefly flickered his direction, he spoke quickly. "I saw what happened. Neither one of you were looking when you backed up. It was an accident, and I think the fault rests equally."

"You don't know what you're talking about," the man snarled. "I was watching. If she hadn't gunned it when she pulled out, my car wouldn't be wrecked, and we wouldn't be having this conversation."

"I didn't gun it, you did!" the woman spat. "And if you hadn't taken two football fields to back up, you wouldn't have even come close to my area."

"Now, wait—" Grant tried again.

"Shut up!" both people said, agreeing for the first time.

Grant threw up his hands and turned to walk away. It wasn't his fight. He'd tried.

Then his gaze caught on a small face framed in the back window of the man's car. A little boy watched the scene, his eyes wide and his expression fearful.

Grant's eyes slid shut. Then, with a soft moan, he turned back around.

"Please," he started again, trying to interrupt the arguing. "What can I do to help? Have you looked at the damage? Maybe it isn't even worth it. You didn't hit very hard. I can check it. Maybe there's not even a scratch."

"Stay away from my car!" the woman ordered.

The man gritted out, "Did you hear me? It's a new car. Any damage is still damage."

"Then maybe I can call the police to come," Grant offered, pulling out his phone.

"No police," the woman said firmly.

The man shrugged. "Police won't come to a non-injury accident in a parking lot."

"That sounds like a problem that could be easily fixed," the woman muttered.

Grant persisted. "Maybe you should just take a few pictures, exchange insurance information, and let the insurance companies figure out who is at fault."

"There's no way I'm giving him my insurance information when this is clearly all his fault!" the woman screeched.

The man growled, "Any insurance info she gives me is likely forfeit or stolen, and there's no way I'm turning this in to my insurance. I'm not taking the hit on my insurance for her stupidity."

Flailing her arms, the woman got in his face and started yelling, most of which was at such a fever pitch that it sounded like gibberish. If the moment hadn't been so tense, and if those little eyes hadn't been watching, the pair of them would have almost been comical. The woman really appeared to be half the man's size in height and twice his size in width. Yet she stood on her tiptoes and punctuated her words with pokes to his chest, making Grant worry about how much the man could take before he really lost his temper and the argument turned physical.

"Wait!" Grant said, trying to put himself between the two.

"If you can't resolve this peacefully, then we'll need some help." Grant fingered his phone. "If I call the police, maybe—"

The woman's fist landed squarely on his chin. He never saw the punch coming. It knocked his head back and sent pain exploding along his jawline.

"I said SHUT UP!" she shrieked. "No police!"

Now quite calm, the man took out his phone and spoke to the woman. "Thank you. I think you just solved the problem. When the police arrive, I'm sure they can now add assault to your list of charges."

The woman spit out a string of profanity. Then, shouting the entire time, she got back into her vehicle. Slamming on the gas, she peeled out and quickly exited the parking lot.

"Thanks for that," the man growled to Grant sarcastically. "Now she's gone, and I won't get anything from her." Then, he too turned, got back in the car and drove away, though at a much lower speed.

Grant reached up and rubbed his jaw, slowly walking back to his own car.

"Hey, Dude, are you okay?" a voice asked.

Grant turned to see a man around his age approach.

"Yeah, I'm fine," Grant said, appreciating that someone was checking. "Though that woman lands a pretty solid punch."

The other man shook his head. "I wasn't about to wade into that mess. I think I would have rather taken a punch from him rather than her, though. She was vicious."

Grant nodded. "At least it's over, and no one got hurt. It really was the fault of both. Neither one was looking."

The man nodded. "I didn't see the accident, but I wouldn't have ventured over there even if I had. I can tell when something is not worth it. You should have just left them to their own mess and walked away."

Grant smiled and unlocked his door. "I almost did. I'm sure

my jaw would have appreciated if I had."

Grant opened his door, ready to hop in and be done with the parking lot.

"So why didn't you?" the man asked curiously. "I was watching. After they lit into you the first time, I saw you start to walk away and then turn and go back. Why didn't you high-tail it out of there?"

Grant paused. "The man had a little boy in the backseat. He was watching the whole thing. When I turned to walk away, I saw him, and that reminded me about a poem I'd just read. It's about not walking away when you see others in need—about stopping when God nudges you—about not being so focused on your own life that you don't see the needs standing on the sidelines. That boy was scared, and no one else noticed. So I turned around, hoping to try to diffuse the situation and get that man back to his son." Grant winced. "I guess I did diffuse the situation, or rather my jaw did."

The other man was quiet, a thoughtful expression on his face. "That's an interesting idea," he mused.

Grant nodded. "I think of all of the situations I usually walk past on a daily basis. I think of all the times when I would have appreciated someone stopping to help me. After reading that poem, I decided I want God to use me to answer the prayers only He hears."

The man smiled and slapped him on the back. "Well, in that case, you'd did admirably."

Grant shook his head. "No, I didn't," he said with a humble smile. "Remember, I almost walked away."

The man looked at Grant thoughtfully. "I think there's a lot of things we all walk away from," he said with a sad smile. "Have a good night. Put some ice on your jaw."

Grant watched as the man stepped away, but before he made it to the trunk of Grant's car, he turned back and called with a smile, "Would you do it again?"

Grant thought a moment, rubbing his jaw. "I guess a bruise to my jaw was worth the cost of ending the standoff. In fact, if the end result was wiping the fear off that boy's face, then I think that's a pretty good deal. But if I had it to do again, I wouldn't do it completely the same."

"Oh really? What would you do differently?"

Grant grinned, the motion drawing his swelling jaw tight. "I'd duck."

Chapter Eight

GRANT knew something was wrong the second Mila flopped in the car and shut the door. It wasn't even hard to figure out. He would have really been a clueless idiot if he couldn't read Mila's slumped, crossed arms and sour expression. Besides, she wouldn't even look at him.

He pulled out from the school parking lot and took his time saying anything. "What's wrong?" he finally asked casually.

"Nothing," Mila answered crisply.

Grant rummaged through his thoughts, trying to figure out his best approach. If he could just get her talking, maybe she would open up.

"How was practice?" Grant asked.

"Normal," Mila responded swiftly.

"How was class?" he persisted.

"Normal."

This was getting nowhere.

Grant let the silence extend several minutes, waiting to see if she'd finally open up.

But she didn't and instead seemed like a statue whose body language clearly spoke of a horrible tragedy its stone mouth would never tell.

"When you're ready to talk, I'm ready to listen," Grant finally said, working to keep his tone relaxed and non-threatening.

Mila didn't respond and didn't say another word the entire drive home. Grant parked the car in the garage and carried the groceries into the kitchen.

Mila planted herself on one of the barstools and propped her chin on her hand dejectedly, watching as he put away the groceries.

Grant let her sit and didn't bother pushing her to help as he usually would. When all he had left to put away were several cans of soup, he took out a can opener, opened one, and dumped it into a pot. It was late enough that he didn't want to bother with anything fancier than soup. Besides, Mila appeared miserable enough as it was. Grant doubted soup could make it that much worse.

While waiting for the soup to warm, he took out the blue notebook and wordlessly perched on the stool beside Mila, figuring that he might as well take these few minutes and start searching through the notebook with a fine-toothed comb.

"I tried it, Dad," Mila spoke up, her voice husky with unshed tears. "I tried it, and it didn't work."

"What did you try, sweetheart?" Grant asked gently.

"I tried that poem." Mila nodded at the tablet in his hand. "I did what the notebook said. And it was awful."

Grant hesitated, startled at the anger now threading her upset voice. "Do you want to tell me about it?"

Mila snatched the notebook from his hand and flipped through the pages. It took at least twenty seconds for her to find the right place. When she did, she shoved the notebook back at him.

"I did this." She said, jabbing a finger at the page. "I did what it said, and it didn't work."

Grant looked down at the page. It was filled with the same small writing as in the front of the notebook, but it was a page he hadn't seen before. It was in the middle of the notebook as if the writer had randomly turned there and started writing before the inspiration wafted away.

> *How many times does something kind occur to me, and I think, maybe I should do that? Little things—like send a card when someone is having a hard time, comment on a Facebook post just to let someone know I saw it. And, yet I don't. The thought gets lost in the shuffle of life, or I think, maybe that would be kinda weird, since I don't really know that person well. Or, I reason they probably have plenty of help and wouldn't want or need it from me.*
>
> *Lord, help me pay attention to those little nudges. If something is kind and the motivation is to help, then it would have to be from You, right? When it is an act of kindness, there should only ever be one answer to the question of "maybe I should." You've answered that already, multiple times, in multiple ways in your Word, haven't You?*
>
> *Yes, I should. I should do it for You.*
>
> *Lord, let me recognize your voice in those little nudges. And if it is in my ability to help someone, even if in a tiny way, give me courage to do it.*

Grant's eyes were wide as he looked from the notebook to Mila. "This is what you were talking about last night."

Confusion clouded her face. "Yes. It was one of the things I read last night when you let me see the notebook. Hadn't you read that before?"

"No, I read other parts, mostly at the front, but I didn't have time to search through the entire notebook, and I hadn't seen this page until just now. Wow, that kind of just sums everything up, doesn't it?"

Mila nodded and folded her arms around her front. "Yes, it does. At least, it sums up an idea that sounds good but doesn't actually work."

"What happened?" Grant asked simply.

Exhaling a long, weary breath, Mila finally explained, "At lunch today, I saw this girl sitting at a table alone. Her name is Alexis Fredricks, but that's about all I know about her. She's in a couple of my classes, but I've never spoken to her before. Then I saw her today, and I realized that I've seen her at the exact table, eating alone, every day I can remember. Every day I've walked past her, seeing her but never really noticing. Then today, when I saw her, I remembered this notebook, and I stopped. I didn't go to my usual table, but I sat beside her and ate my lunch."

"Mila, that's amazing!" Grant said, putting a warm hand to her shoulder. "I am so proud of you!"

"Don't be, Dad. It was awful! I was trying to help her and be considerate, yet the only thing I actually did was embarrass myself. I assumed that she would like the company and would want a friend. But she doesn't!"

An awful feeling knotted in the pit of Grant's stomach. "How do you know? Was she rude to you? What did she say?"

"She didn't say anything!" Mila wailed. "That's the whole point. I introduced myself when I sat down. I then tried to make small talk while we ate, but she didn't respond at all. Even when I asked her a specific question, she'd just nod, shake her head, or shrug. The entire lunch ended up being a long monologue performed by me!"

"It couldn't have been that bad, Mila," Grant protested, sure Mila was being overly dramatic. "Maybe she didn't feel good."

"Dad, come on. I seriously doubt she had laryngitis. In fact, I know she didn't."

At Grant's questioning look, she continued. "I finally got her to say something."

Grant smiled in relief. "See! You said she didn't say anything. Now you admit that she did. What did she say?"

"When I got up to leave the table, I told her that I'd see her later, then she said "bye." And it sounded perfectly fine. No scruffiness from a cold at all."

Grant scrambled for another explanation but came up empty. "Maybe she had another reason."

Mila shook her head sadly. "Dad, she didn't even look at me."

Grant drew a blank. He had nothing left to say to comfort her. "I'm sorry, sweetheart," Grant said, finally giving up.

Seeming to feel her story now had proper support, Mila continued. "And then, after I was completely humiliated when I tried to help, I went outside to find my friends. They asked me all about why I didn't eat with them but ate with that other strange girl instead. And I was humiliated all over again."

Grant was quiet for the space of about a minute. Though he didn't say anything aloud, he was saying plenty to God. He prayed to know how to comfort his daughter, and he prayed that God would somehow honor her efforts and bless her for them.

Finally, he spoke. "That's really rough, Mila. It must have felt like you'd completely failed. But the real failure is if you feel like you were wrong in trying. Sweetheart, I'm so proud of you. You noticed someone who seemed to need help, and you tried to help, even though it wasn't comfortable. Though you can't see any good come from it right now, I have faith that you did exactly what God wanted you to, and I know He will bless you for it. You acted because of God and for God, and that is never wasted. Even though it certainly appears that Alexis didn't appreciate your presence, you never know what God will do in her life because of you."

Mila groaned and covered her face with her hands. "You weren't there, Dad. You didn't see her. Nothing good will come from today. You just don't understand. You don't know what it was like."

Feeling slightly irritated in spite of his best efforts, Grant got up from the stool to turn off the soup. He ladled it into two bowls and set them on the counter. He then took his seat again and said a quick prayer and began eating. Halfway through his bowl of soup, he spoke again.

"You're right, Mila. I don't know exactly what your day was like. But I do know what mine was like, and I have the bruise to prove it." He turned toward his daughter, letting the light fall on his jaw.

Confused, she looked up at his face for the first time since they'd been home. Her eyes flew wide. "Dad, what happened to your face? Are you okay?"

"I got punched," he said casually. "By someone I was trying to help." He nodded to the notebook. "I, too, tried to do what the notebook said. It earned me an uppercut from a very angry woman."

"Oh, Dad! I'm so sorry!" Mila hopped off her stool and ran to the freezer and pulled out an ice pack. She then put a rag around it and handed it to her dad. "What happened?"

Grant gave her a very factual report of the evening. He only omitted the earlier part of his day at work. He saw no need to worry her about that.

"Wow," Mila said when she finished. "I guess both of us should have just walked away after all. We didn't do anything except get ourselves hurt."

Grant shook his head. "Nope. I would do it all over again. Like I said, neither one of us can know what good God will bring out of our efforts. Maybe we will never know. But we both obeyed and honored him. There's never any guarantee that doing the right thing will always feel good."

Grant reached for the notebook and read aloud, *"'When it is an act of kindness, there should only ever be one answer to the question of 'maybe I should.' You've answered that already, multiple times, in multiple ways in your Word, haven't You? Yes, I should. I should do it for You.'"*

His gaze caught his daughter's, and he spoke earnestly, "You didn't do it to feel good about yourself. You didn't even do it for Alexis, though you wanted to help her. You did it for God because you felt He wanted you to show kindness to someone. You shouldn't feel bad because, in every way important, you succeeded. Let God worry about the details. If obeying God costs you some embarrassment and me a sore jaw, then that just may be the price we need to be willing to pay."

Mila nodded. "Thank you, Dad. I'll try not to get discouraged."

"*'And let us not grow weary of doing good, for, in due season, we will reap if we do not give up.'* Galatians 6:9." Grant smiled gently. "I think we both need to take that one to heart tonight."

The rest of the evening passed smoothly, and Grant even saw Mila smile a few times in between her homework and chatting on the phone with one of her friends.

Long after Mila had gone to bed, Grant sat at his desk. He'd gone through the notebook three times page by page. Though he'd found a few more notes jotted here and there, he found no actual clue to who had written it. Restlessly, he'd made a few notes on the story he needed, but he quickly discovered that Susan was right. The story was nonexistent without the notebook's author. Without her, there was no power behind the words, no emotion pushing the story.

Grant put his head in his hands, and just for a moment, he let the discouragement wash over him in waves. He believed every word he'd said to Mila, but his jaw hurt, and his heart hurt, and he was having trouble feeling that those words were true. He felt like a hypocrite. He'd told her that you had to keep trying, even when her efforts appeared to fail. However, at the moment, he very much wanted to forget that he'd ever seen a blue notebook. He wanted to abandon ship on it all—on the search for the girl, the desire to help others, and the whole story.

He didn't just want to walk away, he wanted to run.

Grant's head slid down, and he laid it on his desk.

There was a difference between knowing something and feeling something. He knew the right thing to do, but his jaw told him that it sure didn't feel like it.

Lord, help me! he prayed. *I can't fix this. I can't find the girl. I can't write this story. I can't even manage to help someone without getting punched. Despite what I feel, there are a few things I know. I know You brought this notebook in my life for a reason. I know You desire for your followers to help those in need. I believe that this notebook has a message that needs to be heard—a message to inspire, encourage, and help. If it is Your will, let me be Your mouthpiece and the loudspeaker for this message. Let me find the girl and write the story You would have me. But I don't want it to be my story—it needs to be Yours. I can't power my way through this. I am Yours, and this story is, too.*

He swallowed, his own words driving a shiver of fear through him. He knew that if he really placed this project in the Lord's hands, it was out of his control. If things worked the way Grant wanted, it would be because of God, and if it didn't, it would also be because of God. He needed to be okay with the possibility that he wouldn't find the girl and wouldn't write the story. Then he needed to have faith that, even then, God was in control and would work things for good.

He released a long breath, and knowing what it meant, he whispered, "Lord, do with it what You will."

A Cinderella Christmas

Chapter Nine

Brandi

BRANDI scrubbed at the wall, watching the pencil mark smear into a bigger mess. She sighed. This was going to require more than just a quick fix.

Standing up from her crouched position on the floor, she pushed the disheveled strands of dark brown hair out of her eyes and back toward what used to be a loose ponytail at the base of her neck. Her vision clearing just in time, she dodged the child running past in a superhero cape and went in search of her phone.

Not on the counter. Not on her chair.

She patted her pocket. Not there either.

"Has anyone seen my phone?" she threw the question out to the universe, but it was like a tree falling in the forest with no one there to hear it. Her children didn't even realize she had spoken.

Instead, they were in their own world. Two of them wore superhero capes, jumping over furniture in the living room while throwing a soft football and simultaneously playing tag. Her middle son sat by the front door with Legos spread out in front of him. His face held an intense look that was only broken when one of his siblings ventured close. Then he would let out a loud squawk and yell for them to stay away and stop messing him up. Finally, her two-year-old daughter happily sat in front of the entertainment center, sorting through all of the clam-shell cased movies and spreading them in an ever-widening arc that was now becoming a delightful hurdle for her older brothers playing chase.

"Hey, freeze!" Brandi yelped. Though the kids didn't actually stop, her oldest son glanced her way for about a tenth of a second. "Has anyone seen my phone?"

"Chloe had it," her middle son reported, not even bothering to look up from his careful building.

"Great," Brandi fretted. "And no one took it away from her?" She walked through the living room, peering under furniture, looking in the toy shopping cart, and trying to think like a two-year-old.

"I could use a little help!" she announced, but again, the question whisked away into a black hole and was never really voiced, at least from her kids' perspective.

"Phone, Mommy. Phone." Chloe came toddling up, grinning and patting her belly.

"Yes, where is Mommy's phone, sweetie?"

"Phone, Mommy." Again, she patted the front of her pink overalls.

The beep of a text message sounded nearby. Brandi turned a full circle, her gaze looking everywhere but landing back on her daughter.

Sighing in frustration, Brandi picked the little girl up. Something hard dug into her rib cage.

"Chloe, did you...?" Brandi reached down the front of Chloe's overalls and drew out her phone.

Shaking her head, she couldn't help the smile. This wasn't the first thing Chloe had dropped down the front of her shirt lately. Apparently lacking a pocket for important items, Chloe found a way to improvise. "Were you taking care of it for me, Chloe?"

The little girl jabbered and wiggled to be let down.

Brandi set her on her feet and unlocked the screen to view the text messages.

JAKE: RUNNING LATE

Brandi sighed and shook her head. She had already figured out that her husband, Jake, wasn't going to be home from work on time. After all, he should have been here an hour ago.

Jake running late wasn't new, and unfortunately, she had other issues to deal with.

Bringing up an internet search on her phone, she typed, "How to remove pencil marks from walls."

A few minutes later, Brandi was perusing several different ideas when her oldest son, 10-year-old, Ethan, came up to her.

"Mom, when will dinner be ready?" he asked. "I'm hungry."

"Oh, crud!" Brandi yelped, tossing her phone to the chair before vaulting over the movie cases, and rounding the corner into the kitchen.

"What's that smell?" she heard Ryder ask as she whipped past.

"No, no, no!" she cried as she flipped both the burner and oven to "off." She jerked the skillet with the peas off the hot area, and then pulled the burnt chicken out of the oven.

The peas were so done they had abandoned their green color for yellow, and the chicken was dressed in black.

Tears prickled Brandi's eyes, but she had no time for them. *It's not too bad,* she tried to tell herself. *Maybe if I just cut off the yucky stuff.*

Ten minutes later, she had the chicken dissected, and after the customary argument over washing their hands, she got the kids to sit down at the table.

Grabbing the hands of two of the kids, she bowed her head and said a quick blessing aloud.

"Max, you didn't wash your hands like I told you," she said, immediately after the 'amen.' "Please go do it now."

"But I did!" the five-year-old insisted, a naughty gleam in his eyes.

"No, you didn't. I can feel the dirt on your hands when I held them for prayer. Go now."

"But I can't reach."

"Grab the stool."

"But I don't know where it is."

Deciding it just wasn't worth it, Brandi hefted Max into her arms, walked him to the sink and washed his hands.

Then she returned to the table and cut up meat for all of the kids. Adding some peas and some applesauce to each plate, she called it good and sat down herself.

But nobody was eating.

"Mom, do we have to eat this?" Ryder asked.

"Yes, you do. This is what we're having tonight. If you don't want it, you can wait for breakfast. Look, Chloe's eating it," she said, pointing to the little girl's clean plate. Chloe looked up and grinned, a piece of chicken in her hand. Brandi grinned back. As she watched, Chloe waved the meet in the air joyfully, then tossed it to the floor with great glee.

It landed safely on the floor with all the other meat that had been on Chloe's plate.

Knowing she'd just lost all credibility, she went for the catsup. "It's called Tuscan chicken. It's a new recipe and supposed to taste a little different, but I bet if you dip it in some catsup, it'll taste really good!" she said enthusiastically.

"Can I dip these things in catsup, too?" Max asked, holding up one of the peas as if it were a rather disgusting scientific specimen.

"Sure," Brandi said easily. *Anything to get it down!*

After everyone, including Chloe, had small piles of red magic sauce on their plates, Brandi sat down again and picked up her fork and transferred a few morsels of chicken from her plate to Chloe's.

Out of the corner of her eye, she saw Ryder carefully dip the chicken, examine it on the fork, and then delicately place it in his mouth. Not even a second later, he gagged, and spit it back on his plate with a horrified expression on his face.

She glanced over at Ethan, who had dutifully stuck a piece in his mouth and was chewing, chewing, chewing. Brandi thought his face might be taking on a slightly green hue, and she didn't know that he would ever manage to actually swallow.

Then she looked at Max. He had arranged the pieces of chicken into a row and was pretending the pea in his hand was some kind of bomber as he made another pass.

Something hit her in the ear, and she looked down to see a piece of chicken flop into her lap. Chloe grinned and picked up another piece to take aim.

"Come on guys, it isn't that bad!" Brandi said. Wanting to prove her point, she stuck a piece of chicken in her mouth.

Charcoal. The chicken tasted like charcoal.

She gagged, barely managing to cover her reaction. Two chews, and she swallowed. Then she quickly chased it down with a long drink of water.

"Does anyone want some soup?" she asked casually.

Brandi piled more applesauce on each plate to keep the kids busy—since it was actually the only thing edible. Then she grabbed two cans of chicken noodle soup from the pantry and poured their contents into a pot.

After turning the soup to medium-high, she made sure Chloe was busy with her applesauce and crackers. Then she grabbed some baking soda, water, and a rag and bent down behind the high chair to clean the pencil markings off of the wall.

Thankful, the internet was right, and with a little scrubbing, the baking soda and water removed the markings pretty well. Giving the wall one last swipe with a clean rag to get rid of the residue, she hurried back over to the stove. Seeing the soup sending out steam, she switched the burner to off and grabbed some bowls.

"That's not fair!" she heard Ryder exclaim.

She ignored it. The boys had been conversing at the table for the last few minutes. *Let them handle it*, she told herself. *It's good to let them handle their disagreements.*

She got a ladle and began spooning the soup into bowls.

"You, butler!" Max yelped. "Let go!"

Brandi sighed. "Butler" was what Max called his brothers when he needed an appropriately bad name but knew he would get in trouble for calling them an actual bad name.

"Boys, be kind!" she said, hurrying with the soup.

"You can have that guy," Ethan spoke quietly. "He can fly and use his super vision."

"No!" Ryder yelled. "I had that guy first. And you say he's 100 times more powerful than everyone else, and this guy is only 10 times more powerful!"

"But this guy can fly," Ethan protested.

"Give me that!"

"You, butler!"

"Owwww!!!

Brandi was sure Ryder's ear-piercing shriek could be heard by the neighbors two doors down on either side.

Brandi slammed her ladle on the counter, whipped around, and marched over to the table.

"What happened?" she asked through gritted teeth.

"Max hit me!" Ryder howled.

"He was trying to grab Ethan's guy!" Max explained, eyes wide with certainty that his offense was justifiable.

"That was my guy first!" Ryder protested.

Ethan yelped, "You traded me—"

"Nooooo!" Ryder interrupted with a shriek so loud that it drowned out every thought in every head in the room. "You keep saying that every guy you have is the most powerful. It's not fair. Your guy can't be the most powerful."

Brandi reached over and snatched all the plastic figures from the table. Then she took turns looking each of her boys square in the eye. "Ethan, it's not fair if you always get to make the rules and make them so that you always win. Be nice and treat your brothers like you would want to be treated. Make the rules fair. Ryder, no screaming."

"But, I—" he interrupted.

"No!" Brandi insisted, holding up a hand. "There is no excuse. No screaming. If you have a problem with your brothers that you can't solve without screaming, come to me."

Then she turned to her youngest boy. "Max, no hitting. At all. Ever. For any reason."

Then she looked at all of them. "Do you understand?"

They all nodded.

Turning around, she grabbed a plastic sack from the pantry

and loaded the plastic figures inside.

"What are you doing?" Ethan asked, alarmed.

"You all know you aren't supposed to have toys at the table. You know you aren't supposed to fight. So, these are going to Mommy jail for a while."

"Are we going to get them back?" Ethan asked worriedly.

"Maybe," Brandi said cryptically. "We'll see if you can earn them back by playing together nicely."

What she wanted to do was to toss the sack in the garbage and really make her point. But she knew the boys had only been at loose ends at the table because they'd been waiting for the soup. Despite the anger still rolling through her at their stupid fight over pretend play, she restrained herself and aimed for an appropriate punishment.

Taking a deep, cleansing breath, Brandi got the soup on the table. The boys ate happily while she tried to spoon soup into Chloe's mouth. But the two-year-old kept grabbing at the spoon and wanting to do it herself. Deciding, it just wasn't worth the fight, she let the little girl have the spoon and walked away to get herself a bowl.

Crash!

Brandi stopped and momentarily shut her eyes before turning back around to see the bowl in the middle of a puddle of soup on the floor and Chloe, covered in soup herself, happily clapping as if proud of her accomplishment.

Brandi took the toddler from her high chair. But Chloe suddenly decided she didn't want to be set down and grabbed Brandi's hair with soup-soaked, applesauce-drenched hands. Setting her down despite protest, Brandi stripped her down to her diaper and cleaned up the mess on the floor. The boys finished their soup, and after a stern reminder, carried their plates to the sink.

"Ethan, you need to finish your homework," she instructed as she finally sat down again to attempt to eat a few bites of now-cold soup. Brandi had the bowl empty in record time and cleaned a place on the table for Ethan to set his work.

Turning back around to tackle the messy kitchen, she glanced down at the wall she'd cleaned earlier.

She stopped. Something wasn't right.

Bending down, she traced one of the pencil marks with her finger.

She'd just cleaned it. They had come off, and now they were back on. Brandi's lips tensed as she noticed they were slightly different this time. Darker and with a few more swirls.

"Who gave Chloe a pencil again!" she fiercely demanded.

No one answered. A tree falling in a forest once again.

"Chloe, come here," she called.

She heard the rapid pounding of little feet on the hardwood.

"Chloe, where are you?" she peered around the corner of the kitchen to see a little face smeared all over with something brown, peering around the corner near the front door.

"Where are you?" Chloe mimicked in a sing-song voice.

"Chloe, what do you have?" Brandi asked, hurrying forward to nab Chloe up into her arms.

"Candy!" Chloe squealed, making a run for it.

For such a little girl, Chloe was fast. If not for stepping on the Legos, Brandi would have caught her before she made it into the living room to smear chocolaty hands all over the couch. Thankfully, despite the Lego injury, Brandi was able to perform one more admirable vault over the movie cases and snatched Chloe up before she could take off again.

"Who left the pantry door open?" she called.

"Mommy!" Chloe cooed wrapping her little arms around her mom's neck and tangling gooey hands in her hair once again.

"Hey, where's my pencil?" Ethan asked from the table.

The front door opened.

"Dad's home!" Max yelled, running toward him with outstretched arms. Like in a movie, Jake whisked him up into his arms and twirled him around.

Ryder appeared as well, begging for his turn.

After a whirl of each boy, Ethan called from the table, "Hey, Dad, have you seen my pencil?"

Jake laughed. "I just got here, bud, but I can help you look in a minute."

Brandi just stared at him. Completely exhausted, with her wild hair matted and her shirt smeared from Chloe's leftovers, she marveled that Jake could look so relaxed and unaffected.

"Hi, sweetheart," Jake said to her. "What did you do today?"

A giggle erupted. Then another. *What did I do today?*

With that one little question, Brandi had the sudden urge to bend over and start tossing all of the toys scattered across the floor her husband's direction.

The other option was just to sit amongst the mess on the floor and cry, thinking of all she did and didn't do today.

Chapter Ten

A sudden expression of fear crossed Jake's face as if he realized he'd said the wrong thing. His eyes shot around the room, taking in the Legos he stood on, the pile of movies, the toys scattered everywhere, and the diaper-clad Chloe reaching her arms to be picked up.

"Ummm, I just realized I forgot something," Jake said, subtly hedging his way back to the door.

Brandi threw up her hands in exasperation. He'd just gotten home, and now he was running away. She totally understood. She'd want to run away, too, if she'd opened the door to this mess. But still!

Brandi looked at the sack he'd set by the door when he entered. "You forgot the poster board, didn't you? Jake, we needed that tonight! Max has to take in his "All About Me" poster to kindergarten tomorrow. I have the pictures for it and everything."

Jake wet his lips and looked at her for the space of several seconds. Then he blinked and asked bravely, "Why don't I take the kids and run back down to get it? I remembered the other stuff you said."

He reached the sack out to her. "I got the bread and the carrots. The kids and I will be back in a few minutes with the poster board."

He turned to the kids, urging them to find their shoes.

"You can't take the kids," Brandi moaned. "Chloe isn't dressed, and Ethan has homework."

"I'm done!" Ethan announced. "Do you think my teacher will mind that I used crayon instead of a pencil?"

"I'll throw some clothes on Chloe," he said, quickly taking the girl up to her room.

Two minutes later, he was back down with Chloe clad in a red shirt, hot pink leggings, and neon green socks.

Brandi looked at the clock. "Fine," she said in resignation. "It's time to pick up Alexis anyway."

"Where's Alexis?" he asked, as if suddenly realizing that their oldest wasn't around.

"She went bowling with the church youth group," Brandi reported. "We're supposed to pick her up at the church at 7:00."

Jake's face clouded with confusion. "Alexis went bowling? With the youth group? Our Alexis?"

"Yes, I was surprised, too," Brandi said, raising an eyebrow in amusement at Jake's surprise. "She said she wanted to go. It's discount night, so the youth group went to bowl and eat there."

"I guess that's good that she went," Jake said. "I'll pick her up, and then we'll all head to the store for the poster board."

Brandi offered a feeble attempt at talking Jake out of taking all of the kids. After all, he would be faster with less "help." But Jake shook his head and soon had all of the kids loaded in the van and was off before Brandi could voice any solid objections.

"We'll be back in about twenty minutes," he announced. "That will give you a few minutes to relax."

Brandi watched them leave and wandered back into the kitchen, which at the moment resembled a war zone.

"'Relax,' he said," Brandi mumbled while rolling her sleeves up to tackle the day's dishes.

She appreciated Jake's efforts, but there was no way she could relax knowing that she still had so much still to do. That didn't even include the long haul of getting five kids ready and into bed. Honestly, she didn't know what relaxing looked like.

After she cleaned off the table and loaded the dishwasher, she decided that she needed to use the restroom before doing the hand washing, and she didn't want to miss the chance to use the restroom alone and without the possibility of having the company of children and their endless parade of interruptions.

Maybe this is what relaxing looks like, she thought ruefully.

Though her family had been gone longer than twenty minutes, she hadn't been in the restroom long before she heard the opening and closing of doors and the patter of feet on the stairs.

"Mom!" several voices called as if performing a thorough search of the house.

"I'm in the restroom!" she called, but they didn't seem to hear her.

Soon a knock sounded on the door. "Brandi?" Jake called. "Are you in there?"

"I'll be out in a minute," she answered.

Satisfied for the moment, her search party left, and even though she was done using the facilities, she still eeked out a few minutes of "relaxation" before returning to the homework, cleanup, baths, pajamas, teeth brushing and bedtime stories that would follow.

Deciding that she really needed to gather her courage and get to her tasks if she wanted the kids in bed at a decent hour, she finished up and opened the restroom door.

There, sitting in front of the door was a vase of roses and a box of chocolates. Perched on top of the chocolates was a folded piece of scratch paper that simply said. "We love you. Thank you for being ours." Jake and all of the kids had signed it, including Chloe, whose signature was an exuberant scribble that covered the whole page.

Brandi's throat burned, and a few tears squeezed out of the corners of her eyes before she could stop them. She opened the chocolates, popped one in her mouth and carried the flowers and the candy back downstairs. She passed the candy to Alexis, inviting her to take a piece and share with her siblings. Then she stood on tiptoes and kissed Jake gently.

"Thank you," she said.

"Poster board," he said with a smile. He held up two—one white and one blue. "I wasn't sure which color you needed, so I got both."

Brandi planted another quick kiss to his lips and took the poster board to the table. The next hour passed in a whirl as she helped Max glue the pictures and other things to the poster and got the kids ready for bed. Jake helped more than usual and had the boys climbing out of the shower before she finished the hand washing of the rest of the dishes. With the last tooth brushed, story read, song sung, and goodnight kiss administered, Brandi went back downstairs to find Jake carefully replacing all the movie cases on their shelf only for Chloe to surely knock down again tomorrow.

Seeing Alexis still working on her homework, Brandi asked, "Are you almost done?"

"Yes," Alexis nodded. "I have five more math problems."

"I have to change the sheets on our bed. Come tell me goodnight when you finish."

A few minutes later, Jake came upstairs as she finished putting the pillows in their cases.

"So it was a pretty bad day," Jake surmised, flopping on the just-made bed.

"No," Brandi replied. "It was an exhaustingly normal day."

"My day wasn't bad," Alexis announced, coming into the room.

"Well, that's definitely something we need to mark on the calendar," Jake said teasingly. "Usually all I hear from you is about how awful school is and how mean all of the kids are."

"What made your day good?" Brandi asked curiously.

Jake was right in that usually Alexis was in a sour mood. Brandi worried about her and had thought about taking her to a counselor. Brandi knew fourteen was a tough age for any girl, but Alexis didn't have any real friends and seemed uninterested in doing anything fun or social in nature. Mostly, she just seemed cranky. It had been a tough school year with all of her childhood friends suddenly joining other cliques and leaving Alexis behind. Brandi kept praying and trying to think of ways to help her daughter, but so far, Alexis had just been sour and uncooperative with any of Brandi's efforts. Until today.

"At lunch, I was eating in the cafeteria alone like I usually do, and a girl came and sat with me," Alexis said, unable to hide the shy smile.

"Well, that's nice," Brandi said brightly, shooting a glance at Jake to make sure he heard Alexis' good news.

"Who was it?" Jake asked, readily interested.

"Her name is Mila Dillon," Alexis reported, her eyes shining brightly. "She is pretty popular. But she's also nice. Nobody ever seems to notice me sitting alone, and I thought people just didn't care or like me. Mila usually sits with her friends, but she saw me and sat and talked the whole time. I was so surprised that I didn't know what to say to her. I wish I'd said something."

"I'm sure she understood and wasn't offended," Brandi encouraged, patting Alexis's back.

"She did sit there the whole time and talk," Alexis offered, as if in evidence. "She didn't even eat quickly but spent most of the lunchtime there before they kicked us out."

"See, I told you there are nice people who would like you if you gave them a chance!" Brandi said, feeling her whole body smile with the joy of seeing the sparkle in her daughter's eye.

Alexis nodded. "It really made me think. Nobody made Mila sit with me. She didn't even mind that I didn't say anything. She just talked like I was a friend. She told me all about shopping and a trip she took with her dad. It seemed like she really liked me. I think that if she likes me, maybe others will, too."

"I certainly think so," Brandi said, feeling tears gather at the back of her eyes. "And I love that you're doing such great introspective thinking."

Alexis looked at Brandi, her big, brown eyes soft and solemn. "I think I always automatically assume that people don't like me and don't want to be with me. When someone actually says something to me, I don't say much because I figure what they really want is to get away from me as fast as possible."

Brandi's heart broke, and she wrapped her arms around Alexis. She'd had no idea Alexis felt that way, and she couldn't find any words of comfort beyond her arms gathering her close.

Thankfully, Alexis didn't seem to need any comfort to continue. "Mila didn't act like she wanted to get away, though. She seemed like she almost enjoyed eating lunch with me. Now I think that what I've been assuming about people may not be accurate at all. Maybe there are people who would enjoy doing stuff with me. Or maybe they just wouldn't mind spending time with me, and I'd take that."

Brandi smiled and smoothed back her daughter's hair. "Do you realize I have nothing to say?" she asked. "My incredibly smart and mature daughter figured out some big stuff that I don't think I could say as eloquently as she did."

"I don't think I have it all figured out, Mom," Alexis said sheepishly.

"But you went bowling," Jake pointed out, proving that he was still listening.

Alexis nodded. "I had fun, but I didn't talk much. I guess I'll need to work on that. Wanting to do something doesn't make the actual doing easier!"

Brandi laughed. "That's for sure. Now brush your teeth and get to bed. Maybe Mila will have lunch with you again tomorrow. You want to be rested enough that you can actually say something to her this time!"

Alexis shook her head. "She probably won't be at lunch for the next few days. She is on student council, and they are having lunch meetings for the rest of the week. But that's okay. Maybe I'll get up my courage and ask to sit with someone else."

Alexis was soon in bed, and Brandi turned to Jake, who was flipping through shows on the TV in their bedroom, trying to decide what to watch.

"Thank you for the flowers and chocolates," she told him. "What made you think to do that for me?"

This wasn't the first time Jake had come home to chaos. In fact, she was right in calling it "normal." But Jake's response was different tonight. This was the first time he'd gotten her flowers and chocolates, seeming to recognize her feelings and that it had been a tough day. He also hadn't parked in front of the TV for whatever sports game was on, but he'd pitched in and helped without even being asked, or yelled at, as the case may be.

A calculating light came to Jake's face, and he grinned knowingly. "You're wondering what I've done now that I need to apologize big for."

Brandi smiled back. "Well, the thought did cross my mind. Flowers, chocolates, and help make for a pretty grand apology."

"I'll have to remember that," Jake smirked. "But tonight wasn't an apology for anything." Jake paused as if thinking. "Tonight, I saw a man get punched because he was trying to help two people who'd had a fender bender in the store parking lot. After the others took off, I asked the man why he'd tried to help. Why hadn't he just walked away? He said—"

"Mommy?" a little voice called.

Brandi saw two little eyes peeking around the partially closed door.

"What do you need, Ryder?" Brandi asked.

Ryder pushed the door open and stepped inside the room. "I was thirsty, so I got a drink. And I was just wondering something... Why do they call gophers 'gophers'? Is it because they 'go-fer' things?"

Brandi resisted the temptation to laugh. As maddening as it was, the PJ-clad 8-year-old was quite serious.

She flashed a look at Jake to see if he wanted to handle this one, but he appeared to be experiencing more difficulty keeping a straight face than she was.

"I really don't know how gophers got their names," she answered Ryder honestly. "But I do know that it's way past your bedtime, and you should be asleep. We can talk about gophers in the morning."

Ryder came for one last hug and kiss before he headed out of the room, partially shutting the door on the way out.

"So, what did the man who got punched say?" Brandi asked eagerly, anxious to hear the end of Jake's story with no more interruptions.

"He said he'd read a poem that had inspired him to try to see those who need help—to actually see them and do something about it instead of walking past like he usually does."

Brandi thought, musing aloud. "I guess we don't think about the people we pass every day and what they are going through. I don't think it's intentional. I know I tend to be very focused on my life and the million things I have to do. I probably have blinders on for what goes on in my peripheral vision."

Jake nodded. "He was quite inspiring, especially since his 'help' cost him a punch to the jaw. He actually said that he'd do it all over again if given the chance. He said he wanted to pay attention when God nudged him to stop and help those on the sidelines of his life, even if it cost him. What's really amazing is that he acted so humble about the whole thing, saying that he'd almost walked away instead of responding the way he thought God wanted."

"Wow, that *is* inspiring," Brandi agreed.

"Do you think it's harder to see and help our close friends and family?" Jake asked thoughtfully. "It actually might be easier to focus on helping strangers—people you know nothing about. Friends and family are part of your habits. You see them all the time, so I think it's easy to not actually 'see' them. When I walked in the door this evening, I looked at you, and it suddenly occurred to me how many times I come home and don't see you. Tonight, it hit me. You were tired and frazzled. They probably pushed all your buttons, yet you had cared for them and made sure they stayed alive and were well-fed. I so appreciate you, but I know I don't show it or help you as I should."

Brandi grabbed his hand in hers. "And here I thought you'd take one look at me with my messy hair and clothes and with the house looking like it was inhabited by wild animals, and turn around and run away."

"I wanted to!" Jake answered honestly. "But I think God let me get a glimpse of your perspective, and I wanted to see and help, even if I got punched in the process."

"That's a good thing to work on," Brandi said. "I'm sure

there are lots of people and things that I walk away from, not thinking. I'd like God to show me those people and let me help them as well. "

A noise drew their attention to the door. It sounded like a knock, but not one that was intentional. Brandi caught movement between the crack.

"Ryder, I can see you," she said.

Ryder sat up from where he'd been lying beside the door and stuck his head in the doorway.

"I can't sleep," he said sheepishly.

"I would be surprised if you could sleep on the floor," Brandi responded. "How about you try your bed?"

Ryder picked himself up and came closer. "Well, I was kinda wondering... You know how God made everything?"

Oh, great! Brandi thought. *We're in for one of Ryder's deep spiritual questions that he likes to pull out at bedtime!*

"And you know how everyone sins and messes up?" he continued. "Well, I was wondering why God made all of us when he knew we'd all just mess up and sin?"

Brandi sighed. This boy was remarkable. The way his mind worked never stopped amazing her. But it was late, and she was so very tired. She looked at Jake, hoping he would step in and handle this, but by his avid interest in searching through the options on TV, she recognized him to be fully off duty. Brandi was on her own. Unfortunately, answering these late-night, deep questions was a struggle for her. Despite the hour she didn't want to brush her son off, yet she was terrified of making a mistake due to sheer exhaustion and ample impatience.

"Ryder, do you sometimes disobey?" she asked simply

Ryder nodded solemnly.

"Are you naughty sometimes? Do you fight with your brothers?"

Ryder nodded again.

"Even knowing all the bad things you have done or will ever do, that will never change the fact that I want you for my son. I would choose you, love you, and want you to be mine no matter what. Maybe that's how God feels."

Ryder paused thoughtfully. Then threw his arms around his mom. Brandi picked him up and carried her 8-year-old back to his room. He wasn't a light-weight kid, but Brandi didn't care. He wouldn't always come in after bedtime and ask both silly and deep questions about gophers and God. He wouldn't always need extra hugs and want her to tuck him in multiple times a night. And this was one task she wasn't going to leave on the sidelines.

A Cinderella Christmas

Chapter Eleven

THIS wasn't the first time Brandi had seen the text.

She saw it when it had first popped on her phone several days ago. But she had been busy changing a diaper. She'd seen it later that night when flipping through the messages. But she'd been tired and distracted by the massive mound of laundry. She's seen an email and a Facebook post with the same information. But she hadn't responded to the email or even reacted or commented on the post.

Now she glanced at the text again when scrolling through her messages before leaving for the mall. She felt a twinge of guilt. Maybe she should text back.

Clicking on the message, she read it for at least the fifth time.

> CHELSEY: WOULD APPRECIATE PRAYER. GOT MOM SETTLED AT THE MEMORY CARE UNIT. HARD DAY.

She reassured herself that it was a group message, not one to her personally, and she turned off her phone.

She got Chloe's socks and shoes and headed out to the car. Unfortunately, her thoughts about the text didn't end as easily as the off button on her phone.

The entire way to the mall, she went around and around arguing with herself about whether or not she should text back.

It wasn't as if she weren't responding to a personal message. It was a group text to all of the women in their Bible study class. Brandi knew Chelsey, but she didn't know her well. Chelsey herself certainly wouldn't consider Brandi a close friend. There were other ladies from the group who were closer to her, and Brandi knew they had offered love and support for the challenges Chelsey was facing. In fact, Brandi was sure Chelsey had plenty of help and support. After all, she recalled Chelsey's Facebook post garnering many condolences and comments of sympathy.

There was no way Brandi should feel bad about not responding.

But she didn't hear anything from you.

The thought unnerved her. She pulled into a parking spot relatively close to the front of the mall and quickly shut the engine off. She hopped out of the car, the cold air immediately stinging her cheeks and making her think that snow was on the way. She hurried to pull the stroller out and get Chloe bundled up and strapped in, hoping that the distraction of the busy mall and children's play area would redirect her thoughts.

She quickly shoved her cold hands into her gloves and began pushing the stroller to the elaborate front entrance of the mall. Chloe squealed happily, recognizing where they were.

But it wasn't enough to distract her thoughts from returning to their previous pattern. Frustrated, she tried to talk herself out of the nonsense. She had prayed and would pray more for Chelsey. She really couldn't be expected to do more than that, right?

On the other hand, she hated the thought that Chelsey might not realize that people cared—that Brandi cared.

With her thoughts still in turmoil, she entered the mall and kept walking to the children's play area in the center. She remembered what she and Jake had talked about last night and thought of the countless texts to which she didn't respond or the posts that she read and then scrolled past without commenting, often too busy or thinking that she would do it later when she had the time or could think up an appropriate comment. But she never did.

Now she realized that each time she did that, the writers of those texts and posts didn't know that she cared.

Brandi groaned softly. This wasn't a nudge from God; it was quickly becoming a shove.

She stopped the stroller where Chloe could see the kids playing. She wanted to wait until the other moms showed up before letting her daughter out. She didn't want Chloe to be done playing by the time playgroup started.

She sighed, watching the playground but not really seeing it. What would she say to Chelsey? What *could* she say? Brandi had a hard time knowing what to say when people said or posted about good things. "Yay!!!" seemed a little inadequate and cheesy. But she had an even worse time knowing what to say when someone was hurting. What could you say? It's not like you could make it better.

Maybe just knowing someone is listening *was* making it better.

Even if she did figure out what to say, even if she sent Chelsey a text, wouldn't it be awkward to receive something so personal from someone who qualified as more of an acquaintance than a friend?

Brandi's eyes slid shut briefly. Brandi was busy. Chelsey wasn't really a "friend." Chelsey had more than enough help and support. Brandi didn't know what to say. Maybe it would be awkward and embarrassing.

All of the excuses shoved for top billing in her mind.

Chloe fussed and squirmed to get out of the stroller. She was done with sitting.

Brandi jiggled the stroller back and forth a little, hoping to buy a little more time.

Suddenly, an image jumped to the forefront of her brain. She pictured her daughter, Alexis, sitting at a lunch table alone day after day with no one actually "seeing" her. If they did notice her, maybe they used some of the same excuses that she used now. Then, in her mind's eye, she watched Mila, or a girl she pictured as Mila, start to walk past Alexis's table. But she stopped. Even though she wasn't a close friend, even though she didn't know if Alexis had friends and support, even though she probably didn't know what to say, and even if it may have been awkward and embarrassing, Mila walked over to Alexis and had lunch with her.

Brandi wanted to be a Mila. And she definitely didn't want to ignore a shove from God.

She drew her phone out of her pocket and unlocked it.

"Hi, Brandi!" a voice said. Brandi looked up to see her friend Daphne.

"Hi, Daphne! Just give me a minute. I've got to send this text really quick."

"No problem, I'll be over at the playground," her friend said brightly.

Resolutely, Brandi opened a new message, so it would just go to Chelsey and not to the whole group. She quickly typed.

> BRANDI: HI, CHELSEY! I'VE BEEN THINKING ABOUT YOU A LOT TODAY. I CAN'T IMAGINE HOW TOUGH IT WAS TO TAKE YOUR MOM TO THE

MEMORY CARE HOME. JUST WANTED YOU TO KNOW I'M PRAYING FOR YOU. LET ME KNOW IF I CAN HELP IN ANY WAY, EVEN JUST TO LEND AN EAR TO LISTEN.

She read the text through once. Then, before she could second-guess herself, she pressed "send," and it was gone.

Lord, I did what I thought you wanted, but please help me to not have screwed things up too badly. Just let my message give Chelsey a little comfort to know that I care.

She shut off her phone and parked the stroller, pulling an antsy Chloe out of the seat and carrying her into the enclosed playground. A few other moms had joined Daphne while Brandi was busy, and it looked like almost the whole playgroup was here.

Brandi removed Chloe's shoes and released her to run around the toddler area and play. Brandi looked forward to these playgroup sessions. Several months ago, a few moms from church decided to form a playgroup a couple times a month where their kids could play while the mommies got a little visiting in. Sometimes they met at an individual house, but if the weather was nice, they often met at the park. With it being winter, they'd met several times at the little playground in the mall. It was fully enclosed and perfect for toddlers, having little slides and things to climb and jump on. It was all age-appropriate, safe, and, best of all, free!

Brandi took a seat with the other ladies on one of the side benches that afforded them a clear view of the children playing. Soon, they were all talking about everything and nothing. Daphne talked about some new recipes she'd tried, Gwen told about her husband's new job offer, and Jamie told a funny story about cleaning her son's room and finding an actual snake's skin that he'd added to one of his collections.

In the middle of Gwen talking about a fantastic deal she'd just gotten on kids' pajamas, Brandi noticed a young woman sitting across from them. The woman had dark hair and was sitting alone on a bench watching her son play. Her eyes swerved over to Brandi's group, but when Brandi made eye contact, the other woman swiftly turned away.

Over the next few minutes, Brandi watched the other woman. She would periodically get up and help her son navigate one of the slides. Then she would go back to her seat. When her son looked over at her, she would smile and clap, encouraging him in his play. Then, every once in a while, her gaze seemed to wander back to Brandi's group.

Brandi couldn't read her expression, so maybe Brandi was reading way too much into it—but she wondered… was the woman lonely? Did she wish she could be a part of a playgroup and talk to other mommies? Brandi tried to push the thought aside, but the more she thought about it, the more she couldn't stop thinking about it. What would it be like to come to a play area and see a bunch of other women talking and laughing and not be included?

Brandi tried to tell herself to stop being nosey. If the woman wanted to be included and have friends, she'd just come over and strike up a conversation, right? Brandi looked at her friends. It was probably pretty obvious that they all knew each other and hadn't just met. It may not be comfortable for others to approach and try to be included in an already established group.

Maybe she just wanted to be alone. Maybe she liked it that way.

Brandi rolled her eyes at herself. *Seriously. Who doesn't like to have friends and someone to talk to?*

Alright, God. How about I just bypass the excuses this time and go talk to the woman who is literally on the sidelines?

"Hey, guys," Brandi said to her friends. "I'm going to go talk to that woman over there with that cute little boy. I'm going to see if she wants to join us."

They all looked over and nodded.

"Go ahead!"

"That's a great idea!"

By the surprised expressions on their faces, Brandi knew that none of them had actually seen the other woman before Brandi mentioned anything, but they were ready and eager with their support now that Brandi had pointed her out.

Now, what do I say? Brandi asked herself, bravely walking across squishy carpeting of the play area. Brandi was not a shy person, but she was also not extremely outgoing. She could manage just fine if someone started a conversation with her, but it was far more uncomfortable if she needed to start the conversation.

Just say what you would want someone to say to you.

"Hi! I'm Brandi Fredricks!" she said cheerfully. "I noticed you over here with your cute little boy. He looks like he's about the same age as my daughter. My friends and I come here quite often in the winter, but I don't think I've seen you here before. Is this your first time?"

"Actually, no," the woman smiled. "I think I may have seen you and your friends here before. Maybe a couple of weeks ago? Oliver and I have been coming here a lot since the weather turned cold."

Brandi sat down on the bench beside her and flashed a wan smile. "Well, that shows you how observant I am!"

The other woman laughed. "By the way, I'm Mariana Cruz."

Brandi smiled. "It's nice to meet you, Mariana. I'm so glad the mall has this play area. It really is a lifesaver in the winter."

Mariana nodded. "We moved here a few months ago, so we haven't really figured out what all there is to do in the area. At least the mall playground gives us an excuse to get out of the house."

"Is Oliver your only child?" Brandi asked.

"No, I have two older ones, but they are in school."

Brandi nodded. "I have four older who are also in school." She looked at her watch. "I have about twenty minutes before I need to take off to pick up my kindergartener. Why don't you come over and let me introduce you to my friends? We have a playgroup that meets about twice a month. We'd love it if you want to join us sometime."

Mariana's eyes brightened. "I would love that. I haven't had a chance to meet many people since we moved. Are you sure I wouldn't be intruding?"

"No, not at all!" Brandi assured. "We're just a bunch of moms who like to let our kids play together so we can have a little adult conversation once in a while!"

"Sounds good to me!"

Brandi quickly introduced Mariana, and her friends eagerly welcomed and included her in the conversation. Mariana was all smiles and seemed to thoroughly enjoy herself.

Twenty minutes later, Brandi announced, "I need to run, ladies. I have to pick Max up from kindergarten. Mariana, I have your phone number, so I will let you know when we have another playgroup. It won't be until after the holidays, but I'll be sure to let you know."

"You have all of our numbers, right?" Daphne asked Mariana.

"Oh, yes. I got them all in my contacts," Mariana assured. "Thank you."

"I'll look for you on Facebook and "friend" you," Jamie said.

"Thank you!" Mariana beamed. "I have so enjoyed meeting all of you!" She turned to Brandi. "I have to run now, too. Can Oliver and I walk out with you, Brandi?"

"Sure!" Brandi said. She quickly grabbed a protesting

Chloe, said her goodbyes, and strapped her daughter back in the stroller to head for the exit.

"I guess she doesn't want to leave today!" Brandi said, by way of explaining her daughter's tantrum.

"I can understand," Mariana said, carrying her own son. "I had a great time."

After a brief pause, she continued. "I just wanted to thank you for coming over to talk to me today, Brandi. You really have no idea how much it means to me. All of your friends are so very nice, and it's lovely to be included."

Brandi smiled. "Well, they are your friends now, too, Mariana. But please don't thank me." She shook her head. "Obviously, I should have noticed you weeks ago and talked to you then!"

Mariana laughed. "Don't feel bad. The important thing is that you did today. I had seen you before and thought it looked like a fun group, but there's no way I'd ever find the courage to invite myself over. I've kinda been in a funk lately and feeling pretty sorry for myself. When we moved here, we left my hometown and all my family. I haven't been able to connect with anyone yet or make any friends. I'd decided that this just wasn't a friendly city. People smile, but no one actually cares to strike up a conversation or try to make new friends. It's as if they are satisfied milling around in their own little circles and don't even notice those outside."

Mariana gave a little gasp. "I'm sorry. I just realized how harsh that sounded! I'm simply trying to say thank you! You're the only person who has tried to talk to me and be my friend in the entire four months I've lived here."

Brandi stopped right before exiting through the large mall doors. "Mariana, that doesn't sound harsh at all. Last night, I was discussing with my husband how we sometimes have blinders on to those who may need help on the sidelines of our lives. I've asked God to show me how to notice others and be a blessing to them and their needs. In your case, though I should have done it sooner, I'm very glad to know God used me in your life. And I'm also very happy to have gained a new friend today."

Mariana impulsively hugged Brandi. With promises to text each other and waves calling "Merry Christmas," they parted ways. Brandi hurried through the cold to her car. After buckling a feisty Chloe into her car seat, Brandi stowed the stroller in the trunk and hopped into the car. Shivering, she started the engine and waited just a minute for the car to warm up.

With a smile of complete satisfaction, she closed her eyes briefly. *Thank you for Mariana, Lord. Thank you for the nudge, or shove, or whatever it was that got me to go speak to her. And thank you for not letting me walk away.*

Chapter Twelve

Chelsey

CHELSEY breathed a sigh of relief as the last student exited to the playground for recess. Recess lasted fifteen minutes, and then her students would go directly to PE while she had her official twenty-five minute prep time. Not that there was any time to relax. She needed to look over her lesson plans and make sure she was ready for the Math lesson immediately following PE. She also needed to make some copies, grade tests, prepare her data for the meeting in the morning before school, prepare the supplies for the art project this afternoon, answer a few emails from parents, and move the desks of a couple of students who wouldn't stop talking to each other.

15 minutes for recess + 25 minutes for PE = Not nearly enough time.

Walking over to her desk, she picked up her phone as she sat down. She had a new text message. Curious, she read it and instantly teared up.

Someone had actually responded.

The last few weeks had been so very difficult. Chelsey hadn't been shy about letting her church family and other friends know what she was going through with moving her mom into a memory care unit. Many had voiced comments of sympathy on social media or said they were praying for her. But social media often felt so fake, like an alternate reality where people could say pretend words that didn't require any action outside the little social media world. It was a universe unto itself, and it didn't necessarily intersect the universe of reality.

She'd also sent out a group text to the Bible study group, mostly because at their last session, she had asked for prayer. However, not a single person had actually responded to that message. Until now.

She understood. People were busy. Maybe they assumed others had already responded. She really did think people were praying for her. They had certainly said so at church, and her Facebook post had been quite popular in terms of the number of comments.

But this was different. Someone had taken the time to personally message her, not only offering sympathy, but offering help and an ear to listen if needed.

Chelsey didn't know Brandi Fredericks well, other than through their Bible study group at church, but that made her text even more special. She cared. And that was enough to make Chelsey feel a little less alone than she had one minute ago.

Chelsey pushed a button to respond to the text.

A frantic knock sounded on the door to the playground. Recognizing the urgency, Chelsey hopped up and darted over to open it.

"Miss Simmons, there's a fight, and someone is hurt!" a

little girl in pigtails screeched.

With her own short, blonde hair swinging in her haste, Chelsey rushed out to where the girl was pointing to the tetherball courts. She quickly located the scene of the crime, but it didn't really seem to fit the girl's dramatic description. Three boys stood by a tetherball pole. The smallest one was sobbing. The largest one had a beet red face, was breathing hard, and looked very angry. The middle one looked calm and solemn.

A duty teacher beat Chelsey there and was lining the boys up to get their statements.

"What happened?" Chelsey asked.

"I don't know," the duty said. "I saw boys pushing out of the corner of my eye and ran over.

"You have enough to keep your eyes on out here," Chelsey said, "and you won't even be able to understand them with all the playground noise. I can take them to my room and figure out what's going on. One of them is my student anyway. I'll find out what happened and send them to the principal if needed."

"Oh, thank you!" the other woman said in relief.

Chelsey ushered the boys back to her classroom. When the door closed to the playground, it cut off all the noise from outside, leaving the howls of the sobbing boy to fill the classroom.

"Ok, boys. Tell me what happened," she said, sitting them down at her reading table.

"He hit me!" the little boy yelped.

"It's all his fault!" the large boy said, pointing to the medium boy.

"Let's calm down. How about you start by telling me your names. I already know Sterling since he is in my class," she said, nodding to the biggest boy.

"I'm Lincoln," the little boy said through his sniffles.

"I'm Ryder," the still-calm medium boy responded.

"Lincoln, you go first and tell me what happened," Chelsey instructed hoping that would distract the boy from his crying.

Through his hiccups, Lincoln managed, "We were playing tetherball, and Sterling got mad when he got out. And then he hit me 'cause I beat him!"

"That's not what happened, you liar!" Sterling protested.

"Sterling, calm down," Chelsey said sternly. "Now it's your turn to tell me what happened."

"We were playing tetherball, and I was winning. Then that boy cheated and did a rope," he pointed to Lincoln. "I told him he was out, but then *that* boy," he pointed to Ryder, "said he wasn't out. It wasn't even his business, but he said I was mean and that I should be out. Then Lincoln growled at me, so I hit him. But it was all *his* fault," he said emphatically pointing to Ryder.

Ryder hadn't protested or even seemed to move a muscle in response to either of their reports. More than a little fascinated by this calm child, Chelsey turned to him.

"Ryder, what do you think happened?" she asked.

"Sterling and Lincoln were playing tetherball. Lincoln was winning, and Sterling didn't like it. Right before he won, Sterling called a rope on Lincoln. He said Lincoln touched the rope, but he didn't. It wasn't fair. I told him Lincoln hadn't touched the rope and that he shouldn't be out."

With the calm, precise way Ryder reported, Chelsey believed him. "Did you call Sterling mean?" she asked.

Ryder looked slightly unsure for the first time. "Not really. I said he is always calling ropes on Lincoln to get him out and it's not fair. Nobody else says anything because Sterling just yells at them. It's like Sterling is the boss of tetherball. He makes up his own rules. I told him it was mean to not be fair and make up your own rules."

Chelsey sat back and thought a minute. The other two boys were silent, not really disagreeing with Ryder's report. It certainly sounded like Sterling was being a bit of a bully, and Ryder got tired of it and defended Lincoln. The scenario wasn't too surprising as she had noticed some of the same issues with Sterling in the classroom. He was quite large for his age, especially compared to his peers. He liked to be the boss, and he didn't like to lose.

Chelsey turned back to Ryder, recognizing him as the most accurate source of information. "Why did Sterling hit Lincoln?"

Ryder answered. "He was mad at me. Then Lincoln growled at him, so he hit him instead of me."

"Lincoln, did you growl at Sterling?" Chelsey asked.

Lincoln sniffed a little. "Well, you have to understand, I speak several animal languages. I speak Lion and Whale, and a little Wolf. And tiger. I went like this…"

He curled his fingers up into claws and growled. "Grrrrrrrr."

His fingers dropped, and he explained seriously, "That means 'stop' in Tiger. I was just telling him to stop, and he punched me!"

Chelsey felt a giggle start deep in her throat. She coughed, struggling to keep it down.

Thankfully, the bell ending recess rang, giving her a few more seconds to compose herself. Finally, taking a deep breath, she managed to keep her face straight and responded, "Sterling, do not hit, punch, or even touch anyone else. Lincoln, do not growl at anyone in any language."

She turned to Ryder. "Ryder, thank you for trying to stand up for Lincoln when you felt it wasn't fair. Next time, maybe you can try to go find a duty to help you."

Ryder nodded seriously, but then hesitantly replied. "There isn't usually a duty by the tetherball courts. If there is and someone complains, they usually just make everyone stop playing tetherball."

Chelsey blinked. Ryder seemed to be a very serious, thoughtful boy. Of course, there was a reason he handled things exactly the way he did.

Taking a few seconds to think about the issue, she responded, "How about if I talk to the principal about making sure a duty is close and maybe having the PE teacher go over the rules again, so everyone knows exactly the right way to play tetherball?"

Ryder nodded thoughtfully. "That might work."

Chelsey stood. "Now, this is my prep period, so I'm going to escort the three of you down to the principal's office and tell her what happened. Sterling, I'm afraid you will probably get a call home about punching and hurting someone. Lincoln, you were hit in the stomach?"

He nodded pitifully, grabbing his stomach dramatically.

Chelsey covered a smile. "I think you're fine, but we'll have the nurse take a look at you, and she or the principal will probably call your parents to let them know what happened. Ryder, you're going to come to see if the principal has any questions for you, and then I'll make sure you get back to class."

The boys reluctantly trooped to the office. By the time they got there, Sterling was the one sniffling tears away, knowing he was about to get in trouble. Chelsey gave the principal the condensed version of what happened, and Mrs. Hodges quickly took things over.

Echoing that she appreciated Ryder standing up for someone else, Mrs. Hodges assured him they would work to make the tetherball situation better and dismissed him to go back to class.

Chelsey was still quite curious about Ryder and his unique personality, especially since standing up for the little guy was a quality she greatly admired. She walked with him back to class and couldn't resist questioning him further.

"Ryder, you said that Sterling has been a bully on the tetherball courts for a while now. What made you stand up to him today?"

Ryder shrugged. "He's always making up the rules. He likes to play kids that are lots smaller than him 'cause it makes it easier for him to win. Lincoln has come close to beating him before, but Sterling always gets him out by calling a rope. He's always mean to Lincoln and picking on him because he's so small," he suddenly looked up apprehensively, as if wondering if he would get in trouble for calling someone mean.

Chelsey kept her mouth shut and nodded encouragingly to him.

Satisfied, Ryder continued. "I heard my parents talking last night after I was supposed to be in bed, about how we sometimes don't see the people who need us. They were talking about how God wants us to help others and not just ignore them. I remembered that when I saw Sterling treating Lincoln badly, I've always just let him do it because Sterling is big, and I didn't want him mad at me. I didn't think I could stop Sterling anyway. But today, I knew Lincoln needed help. I needed to try."

They arrived at Ryder's classroom door, and Chelsey turned to him with tears in her eyes. "Ryder, I want you to know that I think you're an amazing boy. I love the way you stood up for Lincoln, and I love why you did it. Bullying is never okay, but standing up for what is right is a tough thing to do, even for grown-ups. If you see anyone else that needs help or any other bullying going on, can you please come tell me? I would like to help, too, and maybe you and I can work together."

Ryder nodded, and his mouth contorted a little. Studying him carefully, Chelsey strongly suspected the boy was trying to hide a smile.

She opened the door of the classroom and stuck her head

in. "Mrs. Richards, sorry Ryder is late from recess. He was assisting us with an issue down at the office."

Ryder started to walk through the door.

"Hey, Ryder!" Chelsey called.

He turned.

"What's your last name?" she whispered curiously.

"Fredricks. Ryder Fredericks."

Chelsey's heart leaped. Fredericks. That's why he looked vaguely familiar.

He was Brandi's son.

Chapter Thirteen

CHELSEY looked at the text for the tenth time. She read it over carefully:

> CHELSEY: THANK U SO MUCH FOR YOUR MESSAGE, BRANDI. U HAVE NO IDEA HOW MUCH IT MEANS TO ME. I WOULD LOVE TO TALK IN PERSON. R U FREE FOR COFFEE SOMETIME?

She quickly pressed send before she could read the text for the eleventh time. She released her breath slowly. It was after school and sending that text had been hanging over her all day. She really hoped Brandi didn't think her strange for asking her to go for coffee. Brandi had offered to help, Chelsey tried to assure herself. Now, after meeting Brandi's son, she was even more sure that Brandi Fredericks was someone she needed as a friend.

After the final bell rang and the students left for the day, Chelsey had sat down, determined to text Brandi back, no matter if she sounded stupid and made a fool of herself.

She had decided to ask to meet Brandi, not only because she wanted her as a friend, but also because she wanted to tell her in person what an amazing son she had in Ryder.

Chelsey's phone beeped, causing her to startle so badly that she jumped.

> BRANDI: I'd love that! Does it have to be coffee? r u a night owl at all? With all of my kids, nights are easier for me to get away. have u ever been to DeeDee's Diner? They have amazing desserts. Is 9:00 too late?

Chelsey couldn't stop the smile. Quickly, she texted back.

> CHELSEY: i am a night owl! dessert at DeeDee's and 9:00 work great for me. When?

She pressed 'send' and waited, literally holding her breath. With a beep, a new text flashed on the screen.

> BRANDI: would tonight work?

> CHELSEY: yes! that would be wonderful! i'll meet u there after i visit with my mom.

> BRANDI: Perfect! See u then! and just so u don't think too highly of me, u don't know how many times I looked at your

MESSAGE AND WONDERED WHAT I SHOULD SAY, OR IF I SHOULD SAY ANYTHING. JUST TO LET YOU KNOW, GOD SEEMED VERY DETERMINED THAT I LET YOU KNOW THAT I CARED! SEE YOU TONIGHT!

Chelsey set her phone down on her desk and reread the messages, in awe of what had just happened. She was more excited about meeting Brandi than if she would have had just planned a date with a guy. Unfortunately, if her last boyfriend was an example of most guys, she would rather have a good friend than a romantic relationship with a man anyway.

Jeremiah hadn't stuck around when the going got tough. When Chelsey's mom went downhill, and Chelsey had to take over much of her day-to-day care, Jeremiah had broken up with her, unwilling to handle the stress of the situation when Chelsey was no longer fun to be around.

Not that she blamed him completely. She knew a weepy girlfriend was not ideal for sustaining a romantic relationship. There was a lot of grief associated with watching someone you love forget. If Chelsey could have, in good conscience, left the situation, then she would have taken off faster than Jeremiah. Nobody wants to go through that.

Chelsey hadn't dated since, and really had no desire to. However, having a friend she could talk to and pray with, someone who would both encourage and challenge her to look beyond herself and her problems—that was appealing. Maybe she was being way too optimistic. But if Brandi's little boy had managed to accomplish all that in one fifteen-minute recess, then she was eager to get to know the actual woman Ryder had eavesdropped on last night!

Chelsey straightened up her classroom and made sure things were in order for school the next day. She ran to the workroom for a few copies and some construction paper. Then she checked her email messages one last time to make sure nothing else needed her attention. Piling a bunch of books and papers into her backpack, she grabbed her coat and turned out the light to her classroom on the way through the door.

Realizing that she'd sent some of her test scores to be printed in the workroom, she stopped there before leaving.

"Hi, Jenn, how are you?" Chelsey greeted, seeing the school's music teacher at the copy machine.

"I'm fine. How are you?" Jenn Murphy responded

"I'm good." It suddenly struck Chelsey how ridiculous this conversation was. She wasn't "good" at all. Why did they always ask, "how are you?" when no one really expected an honest answer. It was a social norm to ask, but it would be socially taboo for Chelsey to actually answer honestly and say, *"Actually, my mom has Alzheimer's and most of the time, doesn't even remember me. I just had to place her in a home because I can't take care of her."*

She sidled a glance at Jenn, wondering if she felt any of the awkwardness of Chelsey's answer of "good." With a jolt, Chelsey realized that Jenn wasn't any more "fine" than Chelsey was "good!" One look at her face told her that Jenn was definitely not fine at all.

Chelsey bit her lip, wondering if she should just let it go. If Jenn wanted to tell her what was wrong, then she would, right? Chelsey certainly didn't want to pry.

Then she remembered Brandi's text. It would have been loads easier for Brandi to not send that text. And then she remembered Ryder talking about how we shouldn't ignore those who need help.

"Are you okay, Jenn?" she forced herself to ask. "I mean that. I'm not looking for the standard answer. You seem upset about something. You don't have to tell me, but really, are you okay?"

Jenn's eyes filled with tears. "No, I'm not okay. Not at all." A sob caught the rest of her words before she could speak them.

She cried. Great sobs wracked her shoulders while tears fell in rivers down her face.

Shocked at her response, it took Chelsey a full second to figure out what to do. Then, as if on instinct, she wrapped her arms around the taller woman and held her. Hearing Jenn sniffle and try to gain control a few minutes later, Chelsey released her, grabbed some tissue from a box on the counter, and pressed it into her hand.

"Thank you," she managed, wiping her eyes and her nose. "I'm sorry. I'm sure you didn't expect this reaction!"

"It's okay," Chelsey said, patting her back gently.

Jenn swallowed. "It's just... I had a miscarriage two days ago."

"Oh, Jenn, I'm so sorry!" Chelsey said wrapping her arms around her colleague again.

"It was early," Jenn said unsteadily. "I was only about six weeks along. My husband and I weren't even officially trying yet. But still. I wanted that baby!"

"It doesn't matter that it was early. It was still a baby. It was your baby."

Jenn nodded. "I hadn't seen my doctor yet. But I knew he or she was there, and I loved him. I was looking forward to holding him, and now I never will."

Chelsey was quiet, simply holding Jenn as she wept quietly. She didn't try to comfort her with words. No words would make it better. She instinctively knew that the standard phrases were exactly the wrong thing to say. She wasn't going to say, *"Maybe it's a blessing in disguise. Early miscarriages are usually because something is wrong with the baby."* She also wasn't going to say, *"There will be more babies. You'll have another one."*

Chelsey didn't have children, and she'd never been pregnant. But she knew without being told that those phrases were hollow and not helpful. Jenn wanted *that* baby. And that little life deserved his mother's tears of longing for what should have been.

Maybe from her own recent struggles dealing with hardship, she somehow knew that the best comfort for Jenn was simply giving her permission to grieve.

After several moments, Chelsey asked quietly, "Jenn, would you mind if I prayed for you?"

Jenn's face crumpled a little, and she nodded. "Please do."

Chelsey didn't know if Jenn was a Christian or religious in any way. She didn't know much about her, except as a colleague. But she bowed her head and prayed for her as if she was a precious friend.

"Dear Lord, I ask You to comfort Jenn as only You can. Please catch her tears as they fall and give her the assurance of knowing that, right now, her baby is safe in Your arms. Help Jenn's husband, too. Help them to share their grief with each other and get through this stronger for having known their little baby for a short time. I know Jenn isn't going to wake up tomorrow to the sorrow being gone. Please walk with her day-by-day. Encourage her and provide others to help and understand. Finally, Lord, I thank You for that little life. I don't believe life is wasted, and even though we will never get to meet that baby until heaven, I thank You that he or she lived. In Jesus' name. Amen."

It took Jenn a full minute to gain control again. "Thank you. I really needed that."

"Jenn, why are you here?" Chelsey asked gently. "Why don't you go home? I can talk to the principal and arrange a sub. You can just tell me what to grab, and I can pull your sub plans together for you for the next couple of days so you can stay home and rest."

"Thank you, Chelsey. Our music program is next week, and there's still so much to do. I did think about staying home, but I really felt that the distraction of going to work was the only thing keeping me sane. If I'm busy with school things, there's no room for me to think."

Chelsey nodded. "I can understand that. Everyone has to deal with things in their own way. If working is what helps you, then you should absolutely do it. But, if you decide you want to take time off, please let me know so I can help. Why don't we exchange phone numbers? If you decide to take tomorrow off, just text me tonight, and I'll make sure everything is taken care of."

"Thank you, Chelsey. I really appreciate all of this," Jenn waved her hand expressively, and Chelsey knew her thanks encompassed everything in the last few minutes.

Her voice still shaky, Jenn continued, "I get so tired of saying I'm fine when I'm really not. I feel like most people don't want to know the truth, and I don't really want to burden them with it. Thank you for not accepting my 'fine' but for truly asking and caring about the real answer."

Chelsey smiled. "I don't claim that I'm always good at noticing others and their needs, but something happened today that changed my perspective." She quickly told Jenn about the fight at recess. She recounted in great detail the part about Lincoln using his animal language, which actually had Jenn laughing.

Concluding her story, Chelsey said, "So after seeing how Ryder didn't ignore Lincoln, I couldn't walk away from you when I noticed you were not 'fine.'"

With one last hug and a promise that Jenn would text her if she needed anything, Chelsey left. She drove home, deposited her bag on the couch and opened her cupboard to find something to eat. Glancing at the clock, she wondered how she was going to pass the time until she went to visit her mom. If she could, she'd go there right now and just spend the whole evening with her, but the manager at Sunset Assisted Living and Memory Care had told her it would be better to keep her visits down to an hour or two until her mom adjusted. They had decided that Chelsey would come after dinner and stay a while to visit, which meant that until it was time for her to leave, Chelsey would do what she usually did—bury herself in schoolwork.

She really did understand Jenn's perspective. Work often provided a blessed distraction from grief.

She put her hand on a can of soup and stopped.

What am I doing?

With sudden inspiration, she grabbed her phone and texted Jenn.

> CHELSEY: Jenn, can I have your address? I don't want u to have to cook tonight. I'm bringing u pizza. Do u or ur husband have a favorite kind?

It wasn't long before her phone beeped.

> JENN: Oh, Chelsey! We both love Hawaiian, but u don't have to do that!

> CHELSEY: I want to. Tell me ur address or I'm going to need to enlist help from other sources. ☺

Jenn soon responded with an LOL and her address. Chelsey quickly placed a pizza order and was soon out the door to retrieve it. After making her delivery to the very grateful couple, Chelsey returned home to happily eat her own pizza. With the leftovers wrapped and placed in the refrigerator, Chelsey was relieved to see that the time was close enough that she could head to see her mom.

On the drive, Chelsey marveled about how good it felt to

do something beyond herself and help someone else. She had been so focused on her own problems lately that she hadn't thought someone else might be having a difficult time and she might be able to help. She couldn't remember the last time she felt as happy and satisfied as she did after helping Jenn today.

Thank you, Lord, for letting me help Jenn. Please show me how and when to help others.

Chelsey pulled off the main street and threaded her way through a few side streets. Tucked into a corner where most people didn't even recognize what it was, a building labeled Sunset Assisted Living and Memory Care unobtrusively resided. It resembled a home more than anything else, and Chelsey knew that daylight would reveal nicely landscaped grounds and an attractive exterior. But she also knew that this home had multiple security features and could not be entered or exited without a code—a fact which helped Chelsey sleep at nights when worrying about her mother.

She pulled into the well-lit parking lot and shut off the engine. With a deep breath and a prayer for strength, Chelsey got out of the car.

She loved her mother but visiting her wasn't easy. She typed in the code for the gate and then again at the front door. Entering the bright great room, she saw that some residents were still finishing their meal at the long table in the dining area. Again, the interior of the building appeared to be more home-like than one would expect from such a facility. The great room featured a large sitting area with a TV directly in front of the door. To the left was the dining area with the kitchen area at a diagonal. Tasteful décor embellished the room in just the right places, making the entire atmosphere feel very homey. With the time of year, the abundance of Christmas decorations made it seem even more appealing, especially with the centerpiece to the living room area being a large, beautifully decorated Christmas tree.

Looking around, Chelsey spotted her mom still seated at the table. Nodding in greeting to one of the employees, she took a seat beside where her mom sat in front of a piece of apple pie.

"Hi, Mom," Chelsey said brightly.

"Chelsey! Sweetheart, I've been looking all over for you!"

Chelsey breathed a sigh of relief. Her mom recognized her. Today was a good day.

"I came as soon as I could," Chelsey said easily.

Glenda Simmons reached out and took Chelsey's hand in two of her warm ones. Idly, she began rubbing it to warm it up, just as she always had since Chelsey was a little girl. "Did you have a good day at school?" her mom asked.

Wow. Today really was a good day if Glenda remembered her daughter was a teacher!

"Yes, it actually was a very good day," Chelsey replied honestly.

"Did you do your best work for Mrs. Munsen?" Glenda asked brightly.

Chelsey swallowed with difficulty. Mrs. Munsen was Chelsey's third-grade teacher. So much for it being a really good day. Her mom thought that Chelsey was about eight years old.

"Yes, I did," Chelsey replied briefly. Then, when obvious that Glenda was awaiting more details, Chelsey added, "We made some Christmas tree cards, and Mrs. Munsen said I did a good job."

Glenda squeezed her hand. "Of course, you did. My girl is a great artist."

Lying was one of the most difficult things about visiting her mom. Up until recently, Chelsey had never lied to her mom in her life. However, all of the articles Chelsey read about Alzheimer's said that it was kinder and better for the patient to simply interact within their current reality. From experience, Chelsey knew that to be true. If her mom's mind was back twenty years ago, and someone mentioned that Glenda's parents were both dead, then she fell apart in grief. To her, such a tragedy was happening right now because she didn't remember. No, as difficult as it was to lie, Chelsey would do what was necessary to protect her mom from the grief of reality.

"How is your pie, Mom?" Chelsey asked, wanting to change the subject. "It looks good."

"Oh, it's delicious," she answered. "This restaurant always does such a nice job."

Clearly, Glenda hadn't eaten a single bite of the pie. And since she still held Chelsey's hand securely in hers, she doubted she would relinquish her hold long enough to eat it.

"Can I help you with it, Mom?"

"Certainly!" Glenda replied happily.

Then, as if it were the most normal thing in the world, Chelsey spoon fed her mom the pie.

Glenda kept up a running chit-chat of random things that really didn't make any sense, but she said "Mmmmmm" and licked her lips every time Chelsey placed a bite in her mouth.

When done, Chelsey set the spoon down and looked over to the living area, wondering if there was room to move her mom over there. As she looked around at the residents, she was struck, not for the first time, by how much older most of them were than her mom. Most women Glenda's age still worked full-time jobs and lived active lifestyles. But for reasons no medical professional could explain, Alzheimer's had pounced early and swiftly.

The first signs of the illness came on about two years ago. Doctors had tried to treat her with the latest medications, assuring Chelsey that they would add years to her memory and her life. Unfortunately, the medications had made Glenda very ill, and she'd had to discontinue them. About a year ago, they had made the tough decision that Glenda should move in with Chelsey. Chelsey's father had left them when she was about two, and he'd never been a part of their lives since. Glenda never remarried, and since Chelsey was her only child, full responsibility for her care fell squarely on her shoulders.

Chelsey had managed to put off the inevitable for as long as possible, but things eventually got to the point that Chelsey couldn't care for her mom anymore. It became dangerous to leave her alone while she went to work, and Chelsey worried she would wander off. So, she sold her mom's old house and made the difficult decision to use the money from the sale to pay for her care at this memory care assisted living facility close to Chelsey's house. Unfortunately, Chelsey was well-aware that with as expensive as the full-time care was, the money from the house wouldn't last forever. She had calculated to the day how long the money would last, and though it was still a long way off, that date kept Chelsey up at night. She simply didn't know what she would do when the calendar eventually arrived there.

She helped her mom out of the chair, and latching onto her arm, she led her to an open couch. Getting her settled, she then sat down beside her, and once again, Glenda picked up her hand.

Feeling a soft touch on her shoulder, Chelsey looked up to see a woman she recognized as Opal.

"My dear, have you seen my Arthur?" Opal asked, her lips tremoring in worry.

Before Chelsey could respond, Opal continued, seeming close to tears. "He was supposed to pick me up so we could go to the bus station tonight, but I've looked everywhere, and I can't find him."

"Remember?" Chelsey said easily. "Arthur went fishing with your son. He said you could both stay another day and go home tomorrow."

"Really? Oh, what a relief! I remember now. Arthur so enjoys fishing with Teddy. Thank you!" Opal happily walked off, leaving Chelsey feeling drained.

It was the same question Opal asked nearly every time Chelsey was here. After the first few visits, Chelsey had started asking the employees about the other residents and learned how to interact with quite a few of them.

Opal's husband Arthur had died ten years ago, but the Sunset employees said they tried to give her a pleasant memory when she asked for him. So far, the story of him going fishing with their son seemed to do the trick. Sadly, like most of the residents, Opal rarely had visitors. This broke Chelsey's heart and caused her to frequently try to pay some attention to residents other than her mom. And it actually did her heart a lot of good when one of them assumed she was one of their family members.

There were residents in all stages of dementia at the facility, and sadly, most of them seemed to be forgotten themselves.

Forgotten.

An idea popped into Chelsey's head and slowly took form. What if she could make the residents feel, just for a little while, that they weren't forgotten?

People were busy in their everyday lives, and just like Ryder had said, *"we sometimes don't see the people who need us... God wants us to help others and not just ignore them."*

What if she could brighten the day for these forgotten ones?

Chelsey talked with her mom for a few more minutes before escorting her to her room and helping her ready for bed, which was all part of their new routine. Then, with teeth and hair brushed and jammies on, Chelsey returned the favor her mom had done so often when Chelsey was little.

Chelsey tucked her mom in bed.

After one last goodnight kiss, Chelsey turned the light out and left the room. With her thoughts racing, she quickly found the assisted living facility office. Thankfully, the manager was still there and listened while Chelsey outlined her idea.

With the manager's enthusiastic approval, Chelsey's idea became a plan.

As soon as she made it out to her car, Chelsey started making calls while her car warmed up. Her first call was to Jenn. She hoped the music teacher would agree to help, but she felt it was probably asking a lot, considering the short time frame and what the other woman already must deal with. Unfortunately, Chelsey wasn't sure what she could do without Jenn's help.

However, as soon as Jenn heard the idea, she gave an enthusiastic, "Yes!"

With promises to discuss more of the details in the morning, Chelsey ended the call. She looked at the time. Since it was approaching 9:00, she drove to DeeDee's Diner, eager to add her plan to the list of things she wanted to tell Brandi.

Seeing she was a few minutes early and Brandi hadn't yet arrived, Chelsey drew out her phone again, excited to make a few more calls. She knew some of her teacher friends from college would be happy to help. Her old college roommate lived about forty-five minutes away, but Chelsey was confident she would be happy to help in some way.

She pressed the number and waited.

"Hi, Emily, it's Chelsey. I was wondering if you could help me with something."

Chapter Fourteen

Grant

ON his hands and knees, Grant scooted the chair back and forth trying to figure out exactly where the infernal squeak was coming from. When he was finally fairly certain he'd located the culprit, Grant applied some lubricant and tightened the screw.

He rocked the chair back and forth again on its wheels, still hearing a squeak, though it was now much fainter. He bent down close to the floor, listening carefully to try to pinpoint the origin of the noise.

"Grant Dillon! What in the world are you doing!"

Grant startled, jerking his head up sharply and knocking it on the chair.

"Owww!" he complained, rubbing his head as he squinted up at Susan standing in the cubicle opening. "I'm fixing your chair! Now be quiet so I can hear the squeak!"

Ignoring his boss completely, he focused on the chair. In about thirty more seconds, he had it, and the chair glided smoothly and silently across the floor.

Feeling stiff from his awkward position, Grant, lumbered to his feet. "All done," he announced.

Susan hurried forward and pushed the chair back and forth herself. Then she sat on it, moving and twirling it around like a child. "You fixed my chair!" she said excitedly. "I've had a work order for it to be fixed for a few months, but a squeaky chair apparently isn't a priority. The thing has been driving me nuts!"

"It bothers you?" Grant asked, curious. Before today, Gant had always imagined, by the sheer frequency of the squeaks, that Susan took perverse pleasure in driving the entire office crazy. It had been only a few minutes ago that another possibility had even occurred to him.

"Goodness, yes!" Susan replied. "It grates on my nerves terribly. I seriously considered just replacing the chair with my one money. Thank you, Grant. That was so thoughtful of you to fix it for me."

Grant smiled. "It wasn't entirely selfless. That squeaky chair has annoyed me and half the office for quite some time. As I was walking by today, I suddenly realized that if it annoyed you a fraction of the amount it annoyed the rest of us, then you needed it fixed. I rummaged around in the cleaning closet and found what I needed to get it done right away."

Susan laughed. "I didn't realize it could be heard outside my office! Even if it was partially motivated by self-preservation, it was kind of you to take your lunchtime and fix it yourself."

Grant nodded, pleased that she had noticed he'd used his own time. "It isn't rocket science." He grinned, "I think I'd walked away from that chair too many times as it is!!"

Susan laughed, seeming to immediately recognize his reference to the poem. "Speaking of which, hang on just a minute, I need to talk to you."

Susan's cell phone rang.

Holding up a finger that clearly communicated that Grant should wait one minute for her to handle this, Susan answered the phone.

Grant stood, idly examining the little Christmas tree again. He didn't want to sit down at the chair in front of Susan's desk. He really didn't want to get comfortable or stay long enough for any kind of conversation. He knew she wanted to talk about his story, and he very much did not want to talk about it.

"He did what?" Susan gasped. "Are you sure? Sterling? My Sterling?"

Understanding that this was a personal call about Susan's son and not a business call, Grant used the opportunity to slip away, hoping that by the time she finished the call, Susan would be too distracted to remember that she needed to discuss something with him.

Grant sat in his desk and clicked a few buttons on his computer to bring up the story he was working on, but it was difficult to focus with Susan's side of the phone conversation still within range of hearing.

By this time, he'd surmised that Susan was speaking with someone at her son's school. Though he didn't know the details, he'd also figured out that young Sterling Martinez was in trouble.

Grant heard when the call ended, and he unconsciously held his breath through the ensuing silence.

He didn't have to wait long.

"Grant, get in here!" Susan called, not even bothering to leave her desk.

Drat! She hadn't forgotten!

Grant reluctantly stuck his head back in her cubicle.

"Everything ok?" he asked cautiously.

Susan motioned him to come all the way in.

Susan waved a hand dismissively. "It's fine. Sterling had a little misunderstanding at school. The principal called to let me know that he'd been doing his work in the office and that he'd stay there for the rest of the school day."

Grant nodded. "In-house suspension," he surmised.

Susan grimaced and shot him an offended look. "It sounds awful when you put it like that! Sterling is a highly intelligent child. If he knows someone is not treating him well, then, of course, he's going to stand up and defend himself."

Grant merely nodded.

Susan sighed. "It may be time for me to look for private school options for Sterling. I'd like to find a school and teachers that could better relate to him and meet his needs. It seems like the incident today was entirely blamed on poor Sterling."

Grant simply nodded, not knowing what to say.

Susan waved her hand as if dismissing the topic and turned a gaze that wasn't nearly so understanding onto Grant. "It's Friday. I need an update on your story."

Grant sighed. There was no point in trying to sugar-coat the truth. "I can't find her, Susan. I've tried everything. The vet clinic is a dead end, at least until next week when the head veterinarian is back. If you need the story by end-of-day Monday, then we'll need to go with my perspective."

Susan shook her head. "That's not good enough, Grant."

"Susan, it's a good story. I wrote it in a way that nobody will even notice that anything is missing. It's touching, and the mystery of the notebook that gave me a new outlook on life is a good angle. It's personal, Christmas-y, and relatable."

"But it isn't a viral, nation-wide story."

Grant shrugged. "It could be. You never can predict what will catch on."

Susan's lips grew taut with determination. "I'm sorry, Grant. I've read what you have so far, but I won't let you settle for anything less on this story. This is what we are going to do. You'll need to make a few adjustments to your story, and then we'll run it tomorrow."

Grant blinked in surprise. "I'm confused. Did you say tomorrow?"

"Yes. We're going to use your story to launch a Cinderella search for your mystery notebook writer. We'll post all of her writing, and I'll get it on every media outlet we can."

Grant wasn't exactly sure what she was talking about, but he knew he didn't like it. "Susan, I'm not going to plaster this woman's personal writings all over without her permission. I'm not even sure about using just her little poem in my story without her permission, but I'm really not okay with using all of it."

Susan impatiently sorted through papers as she talked, clearly communicating that the decision had already been made, freeing her to move on to other work. "Come on, Grant, people will eat this up. From the way you wrote about her, it's clear that your interest extends beyond the professional—and that's good. You'll be our handsome Prince Charming."

"Absolutely not!" Grant protested vehemently. "I am not a sideshow, and I won't allow her to be one either. I seriously doubt that she wants the publicity. She seemed a very private person. Besides, insinuating some kind of potential romantic relationship is completely inaccurate. For all we know, she could be married!"

Susan scoffed. "By the time we find out if she's married, we'll have what we need in terms of publicity. We'll have women lining up to claim the notebook. Of course, we'll leave a few details out of the description so the real owner can identify it."

"I said no," Grant gritted out. "The tactic you describe is in total contrast to the spirit of the notebook. It's about helping and serving others, certainly not for publicity or personal gain."

Susan paused, sizing Grant up and down as if assessing how serious he was. "Grant, I don't think you really have a say in this. It isn't your call."

"It isn't your notebook. Without the notebook, you don't have a story."

"Without that story, you don't have a job."

They stood there in a stalemate, neither wanting to bend or even blink.

"I'll go clean out my desk then," Grant said, calling her bluff and turning to walk out of the cubicle.

"Wait, Grant." Susan sighed dramatically. "I'll make you a deal. We'll abide by my original deadline. You have until Monday at close to find her. If you don't, we'll go ahead with the Cinderella search. By then, I'll be ready. I'll be talking to my superiors. That notebook is not yours. In fact, since you are using it for a story, it is technically under the newspaper's control. Come Tuesday morning, we will do the search with or without your permission. We don't even need your permission to use your handsome photo as the bachelor searching for his muse. You have a contract, I believe."

Grant's jaw hardened, and his words came clipped and forceful. "That's a lot of legal 'ifs," Susan. You may win, but you may not. If you want to test the legal waters, the only thing you can really count on is that I will make it difficult enough that you won't be raising a victory flag in time for your Tuesday contest. The legal system does move rather slowly, don't you think?"

Susan's mouth puckered as if she'd tasted a lemon. "We shall see."

Grant started to leave and paused. He spoke quietly "Susan, my search for the notebook's owner is personal, not for public scrutiny."

She didn't even look at him again but replied in a casual,

off-hand way. "Grant, you made it public when you decided to write a story about it. That decision was all yours. It's a little late to try to change the rules."

Grant left the cubicle, flopped into his desk chair, and took deep, cleansing breaths, trying to resist the urge to throw something. This wasn't the first time he and Susan had faced off, but this was the worst. Grant knew that Susan's methods weren't inhibited by the same ethics Grant practiced. But this was low, even for her. She had both threatened to fire him and said that, even without their permission, she would use Grant and his mystery woman for her publicity stunt.

All that was after he'd fixed her chair.

Lord, I need some help! I'm in a mess here, and I don't know a way out! I shouldn't have ever mentioned the notebook to Susan. I guess I was desperate for a story that would get her off my back, and now I have the awful feeling that I've cast pearls before swine. If you can help me find the writer of the notebook, I will still try to do the right thing and write the story in a way that doesn't commercialize the message, but glorifies You.

"Grant! Get in here!" Susan's voice rang out again.

Grant shut his eyes. He really wasn't up for another round with Susan.

Reluctantly, he stood and obediently reentered her cubicle.

"Yes?" he asked stiffly.

"I need you to cover a story. Some local teachers are taking their students to a nursing home to bring some joy to the residents. They are singing and giving gifts and cards. It's tonight. This paper has your info, including the name of the organizer." Susan handed him a paper.

"And why...?" Grant started to ask, and then stopped. Maybe he shouldn't say anything. "Do we usually cover nursing home programs?"

Susan looked up impatiently. "It's Christmas. We're short on feel-good stories. I'd assign another reporter, but I need the story to actually be good and not boring. You shouldn't have trouble finding a good angle. I'm not looking for a news story on the program; I'm looking for something of the more human-interest variety, which you claim is your specialty. With your reluctance with your other assignment, I didn't think you'd mind. Boring little local stories is what you like most."

"No, I don't mind," Grant assured, ignoring the barb. "I just like knowing what my actual assignment is and the reason behind it."

"I need it for the paper tomorrow," Susan said flatly. "Email it to me tonight. I need to have something to liven up all the shopping advertisements in tomorrow's edition."

Grant returned to his desk and glanced at the information on the paper Susan had given him. The organizer was Chelsey Simmons, and the event was supposed to start at 7:00.

Susan was right. He did like this type of assignment. It was like searching for a diamond in what everyone else thought was a field of dirt. This wasn't the story he wanted to be writing, but he needed to let the Lord handle that one. For now, he fully intended to find a diamond at Sunset Memory Care and Assisted Living.

Chapter Fifteen

"**COME** on, Dad!" Mila moaned. "Can't you please just take me home first?"

"I already told you 'no,' Mila," Grant replied, pulling into a parking spot at the assisted living facility. "Now stop asking."

Mila folded her arms across her front. "This is totally not fair. It's not like it's 'take-your-kid-to-work' day."

Grant sighed. His daughter was an amazing person, but she was still a teenager. And some days she seemed more of a teenager than others.

Before opening his car door, Grant turned and looked at her directly. "Mila, I wanted you to come for several reasons. First of all, I didn't have time to run you home after basketball practice and still make it on time for the event. Second, this program is about bringing joy to people who don't have a lot of opportunities for joy and visitors. I want you to see people helping and serving others, and if you want to participate, then I think that would be great. Finally, I wanted you to come because I like being with you. It shouldn't take long for me to get enough info for a story, but after we're done, I need to go home and write it. Since that won't give us a lot of time to spend together tonight, I didn't want to miss more when there is no reason why you can't go with me."

"Fine," Mila responded, though clearly unwilling to give up the pouty lip and admit to being appeased.

Grant got out of the car and went to the front gate with Mila following behind. An employee already stood in position letting people through.

Grant blinked in surprise when he stepped into the facility. This wasn't a little, somber event. Noise filled the room, but it wasn't chaotic; it was happy, organized noise. All of the residents were seated in the living room area. More chairs had been brought in so visitors had seats as well with a few extras, just in case. The elderly audience sat positioned in a semicircle around the fireplace, and their eyes were bright and already fixed in delight on a group of children standing to one side of the fireplace.

Grant quickly found a seat for Mila and himself. He didn't have long to wait before a woman came to the front and introduced the students. Soon the room filled with the sound of little voices singing "Up on the Housetop." What followed was one of the cutest mini-music programs Grant had ever seen. Every child knew every word and each accompanying action. It was obvious that they thoroughly enjoyed the attention as their audience clapped and grinned in all the right, and in some of the wrong, places.

After an adorable version of "We wish you a Merry Christmas" as a finale, the woman who spoke earlier came back to center stage and explained that the children had all brought presents and cards for the residents. The children would distribute their gifts and then help decorate the tree and serve cookies.

Grant watched in amusement as the children each delivered a Christmas gift. When the elderly recipient had difficulty opening the wrapping paper, he or she would urge the child to help. Only too eager to help unwrap a present, the child sent the paper flying to reveal a little handmade ornament in each package. Then, often hand-in-hand, the two would take the ornament over to the tree and carefully hang it.

"Hi, Mila," a soft voice said quietly.

Grant turned to see a dark-haired girl who looked to be around Mila's age hesitantly standing directly behind them.

"Hi," Mila replied, looking surprised.

"How were your student council meetings?" the other girl asked.

"They were good," Mila replied. "Why are you…?"

"My mom is here helping out, and she made me tag along," the girl said.

"Yeah, that's kinda why I'm here, too," Mila said, shooting a wary glance up to her dad.

The girl's eyes brightened, "Hey, Mom wants me to take some pictures. She even gave me her phone. Do you want to help?"

"Sure!" Mila said with a smile. "Dad, can I borrow your phone?" she asked, holding out her hand expectantly.

"Your dad won't let you have a phone either?" the girl asked excitedly. "I thought I was the only one at school who didn't have one."

"Oh, I have a phone. But it's a really old one I think they used in the days of the dinosaurs. Plus, my dad has everything but the actual phone part restricted. He says it's only for emergencies, so I can't even use the camera unless he changes the settings."

Grant handed her the phone. "Who is your friend?" he asked pointedly.

"Oh, this is Alexis, Dad."

"Did you say Alexis?" Grant asked, surprised.

Mila nodded. "Yes, Alexis Fredericks. Remember, I told

you we had lunch together the other day."

"I remember. I just didn't know if I heard right. It's not as *quiet* as I thought it would be in here." He wiggled questioning eyebrows at Mila.

She shrugged slightly and tried to conceal a sheepish smile. Apparently, Alexis wasn't as quiet as she thought either.

"You and Alexis go take some pictures. I need to interview a few people," Grant said, turning to look around the room and locate the person in charge.

Many kids and residents were still busy decorating the tree or eating cookies. Seeing the woman who had made the announcements, Grant walked over and held out his hand. "Hi, I'm Grant Dillon from *The Brighton Daily*. Are you Chelsey Simmons?

"Yes, I am!" she said, eagerly shaking his hand. "Thank you so much for coming, though I have to say it was a surprise. I didn't really anticipate our little party would be a Grant Dillon-worthy event."

Grant smiled. "Watching paint dry can be a Grant Dillon-worthy event. It just depends on how the story is told."

Chelsey laughed. "Well, good! Hopefully, we're a step up from paint drying!"

"You're the one who organized all of this?" Grant asked, getting down to business and taking out a little notebook to jot a few notes.

"Yes, I organized it, but I had a lot of help," Chelsey explained. "Jenn Thomas is the music teacher at the school where I teach. She brought a group of her students to do the little performance. My friend Brandi Fredericks has been such a help with everything as well. She helped many of the students make the cards and gifts. However, students from my school aren't the only ones who participated. A few of my other teacher friends were unable to bring their students tonight, but they still sent ornaments and cards." She turned and touched the elbow of a woman standing close by. "Hey, Brandi! Have you seen my friend Emily? I saw her here a little while ago dropping off things her class had made. Maybe Mr. Dillon would like to talk to her as well."

"Brandi looked around at the crowd. "I know she said she couldn't stay long because she needed to get back home, but I thought I saw her a moment ago talking to some of the kids."

Not really feeling the need to track down someone else to speak with, Grant asked Chelsey, "What gave you the idea for tonight?"

Chelsey hesitated. "My mother is a resident here. In fact, I just moved her in recently, so I come here every day. I'm still getting to know some of the other residents, but I have observed that there aren't many other visitors who come. I understand why. Visiting is difficult. My mom has Alzheimer's and doesn't remember me at all sometimes. But even though they can't remember, they can still feel. I want to give them some joy and maybe a little comfort to know that though they have forgotten, they are not forgotten."

Grant nodded. "That's a beautiful thought. Did the idea just occur to you? Have you been planning it for long?"

"No," Chelsey answered, again hesitantly.

Grant got a familiar feeling. Chelsey had a story, and for some reason, she was a bit reluctant to share it.

Chelsey looked over to her left, almost as if looking to someone else for permission to share.

Grant followed her gaze to her friend Brandi. Suddenly, movement caught his eye with a flash of blonde hair and the face that had been haunting his dreams.

It can't be her, he told himself.

As if in the background, he heard Chelsey speak. "You really might want to talk to Brandi about her side of the story. She'd probably tell it better than me. For my part, the day I got the idea, there had been a bit of a fight between three boys at school…"

Chelsey's words continued, but Grant had already lost track.

It just can't be… He scanned the crowd, trying to catch another glimpse, but it was as if her image had taunted him, and she melted out of view.

"Excuse me," Grant mumbled. "I'll be right back."

Grant hurried in the direction that he'd seen her, growing more frantic by the second.

Most of the heads around him were white or silver, and he couldn't catch sight of a single blonde. Even if it wasn't her, he'd feel better if he just confirmed that the woman he'd seen was not his mystery notebook writer.

"Excuse me," he said, catching the attention of one of the employees. "Did you see a blonde woman come this way?"

She shook her head. "Sorry, I've been focusing on the ones who haven't boasted blonde hair in many years! Tera over there has blonde hair, at least currently. She's one of our employees. Is she the one you're looking for?"

Grant shook his head. Tera was a heavy-set woman in her late forties wearing bright purple scrubs and a sour expression. She was definitely not who he was looking for.

Grant made a complete circle around the large room twice, but the face he had seen had disappeared. Coming to his senses enough to realize how he must look to the woman he was supposed to be interviewing, he reluctantly headed back to the fireplace area.

Still scanning faces, he suddenly froze. But it wasn't the familiar face of a woman that gave him pause. Sitting on the couch was the same elderly man he'd seen at the vet clinic. Nestled up beside him was an elderly woman. They were both smiling happily and holding hands as they watched a child who seemed to be acting out something quite dramatic with several ornaments swinging around his fingers.

Grant found Chelsey and immediately pointed to the couple. "Do you know that couple sitting on the couch?" he asked.

"Oh, yes! That's Henry and Pamela Garinger. Pamela is a resident, and Henry comes to visit her every day. I think he and I are the only daily visitors. Aren't they a sweet couple? Pamela doesn't always remember his name, but she always holds his hand."

Grant felt shock race down his spine as he remembered how Henry kept saying at the vet clinic that he needed to call his wife. It just about broke his heart all over again to know that the poor, lonely man had desperately wanted to talk to his wife in his hour of need. Even though she wouldn't have been able to offer a true opinion and there was no guarantee that she'd even know his name, he'd still longed for the comfort of his wife.

Grant eagerly turned to Chelsey, "Miss Simmons, I really want to hear the rest of your story of how you came up with the idea for tonight, but I also want to go talk to Henry and Pamela. Seeing how they care for one another, I have a feeling they might have a story that could be very touching if I can manage to combine it with tonight and your reasons for doing this event."

Chelsey smiled. "Mr. Dillon, if you can manage to paint that picture with words, I think you will have a beautiful story."

For just a second more, Grant savored the picture Chelsey was referring to, committing it to memory. It was the image of the elderly couple sitting close, hand-in-hand, and beaming at a child who had now donned Pamela's lap blanket as a cape to continue his performance. All in one, it was the embodiment of past, future, and everything Christmas should be in the now.

It was at that exact moment that Grant gave up. It wasn't a sad feeling. It didn't even feel like he'd failed. But he knew he wouldn't look for the woman anymore.

Susan was wrong. He didn't need the woman to

communicate her message. He didn't even need the notebook. What he needed was a story that spoke of love, sacrifice, serving others, and recognizing those needs and people who are often forgotten.

Though it wasn't the story he'd originally intended to write, Grant knew he'd found his story. And Miss Simmons was right. It was beautiful.

Chapter Sixteen

Emily

SNOW fell in a thick, cascading veil obscuring the world beyond a few steps in front of Emily's feet. She hurried through the parking lot to her car, part of her wishing she hadn't made the trip to Brighton Falls this evening. She didn't like to make the drive in the middle of a sunny day, and she especially didn't like to drive at night. Now she needed to navigate home in the dark and snow, which she really, really didn't like. Overwhelmed with dread, she seriously worried that her nerves wouldn't survive.

But the other part of her felt rather proud of herself. Coming tonight and delivering the ornaments and cards her students had made for the assisted living home had been important. She knew it was important for her friend, Chelsey, and she knew it was important to the residents who, as Chelsey said, deserved to know that they weren't forgotten.

Even though it was difficult and had required a serious

battle with her anxiety, Emily had made the delivery, knowing exactly what it would cost her.

While she really couldn't feel bad about coming, she did regret stopping at the store. She should have just gone directly home after spending a few minutes at Sunset, but her bare cupboards required just a few occupants. She thought if she stopped really quick for some groceries here in the city, then she wouldn't need to do it once she made it back to her own town.

Now, heavily-laden with plastic sack handles threaded in her fingers, she hurried to her car, hoping that she could still make the 45-minute drive home to Crossroads before the roads got really bad.

Unfortunately, she didn't even make it to her car. With a sickening rip, the flimsy sacks tore out the bottom, and her groceries plopped into the slush of the parking lot. Unable to stop herself, Emily's tears quickly joined the snow in sliding down her cheeks to join the groceries on the wet cement.

Having no more intact sacks to carry her things the rest of the way to her car, she hurriedly piled everything she could into her arms. But she couldn't fit it all.

She looked at her car that was still at least twenty feet away. Then she looked back to the store, which was about thirty feet away. Whatever she did, she would need to leave some of her groceries in the middle of the parking lot while she ran one load to safety. She could come back for another load, but it was so wet and dark that there was a good chance a car would just run over the groceries in the middle of the parking lot without even seeing them.

She had pushed her hood back to see as she bent over the groceries. Now her hair was wet, and her pant legs and coat were soaked from bending down to gather the things and cradle them against her front.

Deciding that making a run for it was her only option, she grabbed a couple more cans and stood. But the movement caused a few small boxes on the bottom of her pile to slide and fall back to the ground.

She picked two of the boxes up again and took a step. A can of soup slipped from her hand and landed on her foot.

A woman in high heels walked past, hurrying to her car.

Emily didn't pick up the soup can but stepped forward, deciding to make it to her car and make several trips back, hoping for the best.

Another can of soup fell and rolled across the concrete.

The high-heeled woman in front of her suddenly stopped and turned around. Taking a few steps back, she bent and retrieved the soup can.

"I have some extra reusable bags," the woman said, holding out a green canvas bag. "Let's put your groceries in the bags, and I'll help you carry them to the car."

"Thank you!" Emily said, sniffling.

They quickly loaded everything up in three of the woman's bags. Emily led the way to her car and opened the trunk. Hurriedly, she started unloading the groceries into the trunk so she could give the bags back to the kind woman.

"Oh, just keep them," the woman said. "You'll need them to carry your things inside after you get home, and I have plenty more."

"Can I pay you for them?" Emily asked, quickly.

"No, not at all," the woman replied cheerfully. "They're yours. Have a Merry Christmas."

The woman started to head back to her car. Emily called, "Thank you! I don't know what I would have done without your help."

The woman paused and turned back around. For several seconds, she just stood thoughtfully in the snow, as if thinking. Then she smiled and said, "Please don't thank me. I almost walked away."

Emily startled.

Her mouth opened and closed, but no sound came out. She wanted to stop the woman again and ask her what she meant, but before Emily could untangle her tongue, the woman got in her car and drove away.

Emily slid into the driver's seat of her car and sat, stunned for several minutes.

She said she almost walked away. Just like my notebook.

My notebook!

Emily grabbed her purse and frantically unloaded it, looking for her notebook. But it wasn't there.

Where did I leave it?

She took a deep breath and closed her eyes, thinking back to the last time she had the notebook.

The vet's office! I must have left it at the vet's office!

With a groan, she realized it was Friday. The vet clinic was closed and would be until Monday. The first time she would be able to check at the office and pick the notebook up would be Monday. Since she had to teach, she couldn't do it until after school. Then it would be a mad dash to drive to Brighton Falls again, hoping that the office still had her notebook.

Emily drove home, battling her thoughts the whole way. She alternated between anxiety over driving at night in the snow and thoughts over her notebook. She told herself that it was just a coincidence that the stranger had used the same phrase she had written about in her notebook. However, inevitably her thoughts would drift back to wondering why she had used that particular phrase.

Then she'd realize that her mind had drifted while she was driving, and she would freak out that maybe she wasn't paying close enough attention to the road. She would readjust and try to empty her mind of everything but the road in front of her.

Then her mind would gradually wander back to her notebook and the stranger, causing the cycle to start over again.

She eventually made it home and even made it to church sunday. however, through the rest of the weekend, she had trouble tearing her thoughts away. Even though she was sure it was just a coincidence that God had simply used the phrase to remind her of her notebook, she still felt restless.

As soon as she could leave for the day on Monday, Emily left the school and drove to Brighton Falls yet again. She arrived at about 4:40, which was only twenty minutes before the office closed. She just needed to pick up her notebook, though, so she hoped that would be plenty of time.

She walked into the office and waited for another person to take his turn picking up his dog. Though she knew it wouldn't still be there, she glanced at the chair she'd sat in exactly one week ago. Of course, there was nothing on or under the chair, so Emily waited.

When it was her turn, Emily stepped forward and spoke to the same surly receptionist who had been working last week. "I was here a week ago to pick up my mom's bulldog," Emily explained. "I think I left a small, blue notebook under the chair where I was sitting. Have you seen it?"

The other woman shook her head before Emily had even finished speaking. "I'm sorry. I don't recall anything that was left here. Have you checked your car?"

Emily bristled at the condescending remark. "I know I left it here. Can you please look? It was last Monday. It was the same evening that one gentleman's dog attacked another dog, and they were trying to decide about surgery. I think another man was here along with the older two men, but he sat on one of the chairs waiting."

"Look," the receptionist said irritably. "I don't have time to play hide and seek with a noteb— "

Her eyes suddenly flashed in what looked like recognition. "Wait a minute. Did you say it was a *blue* notebook? Was it one of those smaller spiral-bound notebooks you can get for less than a buck?"

"Yes!" Emily cried. "That's it!"

The receptionist immediately began searching through piles all over the desk and counters. "Where is it?" she mumbled, talking to herself as Emily waited breathlessly. Thankfully, there was no one else in the office after the man with the dog left. After several minutes of searching fruitlessly, Emily began to worry that they had lost her notebook permanently.

The receptionist literally got on the floor under the desk and began shuffling through more papers.

Just when Emily was about to ask if she could come behind the desk and help look, the receptionist called gleefully. "I found it!"

She stood from the floor and handed the business card to Emily.

Confused, Emily took the card and stammered, "But this isn't my notebook!"

"Oh, we don't have your notebook. One of the other men who was here that night found your notebook and took it for safe-keeping. He said that if you came looking for it to give you his card and you could pick it up. I think he works at a newspaper or something like that. He wanted me to give him your contact info, but of course, I wouldn't do that. He even called the next day still asking for it, but I wouldn't budge. Of course, I didn't even know your name or contact info to give him, but still."

"Grant Dillon," Emily mused, looking at the card. "I think he's a reporter. I've read some of his stories. It looks like he works at *The Brighton Daily*." She glanced at the time. "Oh no, I've got to run! They probably close at 5:00."

Emily hurried out the door but then stopped with the door

open. "What happened to the dog?" she asked hurriedly.

"What?" the receptionist asked, clearly not following.

"What happened to the dog that was attacked by the other dog a week ago? Did he have surgery? Did he live?"

It was as if the woman pulled a thick veil over her features. "I'm sorry," she said, her tone full of superiority. "I am not at liberty to discuss patient information. There are confidentiality laws, you know. HIPPA isn't just for people."

Emily blinked. "I'm sorry. I didn't realize. I just wanted to know if the dog was okay. Thank you for your help."

Emily shut the door and hurried to her car. Several minutes later, she pulled into the parking lot at *The Brighton Daily*.

She looked at the time. Two minutes. It was 4:58. She wasn't going to make it.

She jogged into the building, trying to avoid the potentially icy spots in the parking lot. She pushed open the door and hurried to the front desk.

Out of breath, she struggled to speak. "I need to speak with Grant Dillon," she managed.

"I'm not sure he's available," the receptionist hedged. "We are closing, and I know he had some meetings and a deadline. Maybe I can get another reporter or someone else can help you quickly."

"Please, it needs to be Mr. Dillon. If I can just talk to him for thirty seconds, I'll get out of his way. I live forty-five minutes away, and I'm a teacher. It would be extremely difficult for me to make it back during business hours."

The receptionist took out a piece of paper. "Can I take a message for you? Maybe Mr. Dillon can just call you back and save you a trip."

"Not really," Emily said, her voice wavering unsteadily. "I think he has my notebook, and I just need to get it back."

The woman's pen dropped, and she stared at Emily. "Did

you say that Grant has your notebook?"

Emily nodded emphatically. "Yes. He picked it up when we were at the same vet clinic last week. The vet's office gave me his card and said he had it."

"Come with me right now," the woman said.

Emily followed the receptionist through a door behind the desk. As if wanting to keep track of Emily, she gently put a hand on Emily's arm, guiding her through the hallway.

Emily recognized Grant as soon as she saw him. He sat at a desk with a pensive look on his face. His dark hair waved away from his face, and his strong jaw held a bit of tension. Emily remembered seeing his picture in the paper and remembered thinking what a handsome man he was. Emily must have been too stressed last week at the vet's office to recognize who he was. She now remembered him sitting a few chairs over from her, but she hadn't given him any kind of inspection at the time.

Before the receptionist said a word, Grant looked up.

His eyes met Emily's, and he stood. His face went pale.

"It's you!" he whispered.

Not knowing how to respond, Emily extended her hand. "I'm Emily Jansen. Pets and Vets Specialty Hospital gave me your card and told me you had my notebook."

"I'm sorry, Grant," the receptionist beamed. "I know you didn't want to be interrupted, but I thought this might be an exception. I already tried to send her away before I figured out who she was."

Grant swallowed. "Thank you, Wendy."

"You do have my notebook, don't you?" Emily asked. "I know you're busy. I can just hurry and be on my way."

"Yes, I have it," Grant said. He took the notebook from his briefcase, but he didn't hand it to her. He looked at it, then back to her, holding the spiral pad gently.

He seemed unsure of what to say, and the whole experience

was becoming more and more confusing for Emily.

Grant cleared his throat and looked nervously in the direction of a nearby cubical. Quietly he spoke. "I was wondering if I could take you to coffee. I'd like to talk to you a few moments about your notebook."

Emily looked around, noticing the many eyes who looked at her with open curiosity. She seemed to be in the spotlight for the entire office. Everyone she saw stared in her direction or had stopped working entirely. Some were even sticking their heads out of their cubicles to watch.

"Umm, why is everyone looking at me?" she whispered nervously.

Grant leaned forward and spoke again for her ears only. "I can explain everything over coffee if you'll let me. I really don't want to talk to you with an audience."

A sudden thought struck Emily, and though it was completely off the subject, she asked anyway. "Do you know what happened to the dog at the vet clinic? Do you know if he had surgery or if he lived? It's been really bothering me. I tried to ask the receptionist, but she wouldn't tell me what happened. You were there after I left, weren't you? Do you know what happened?"

"The dog lived," Grant said simply.

"Oh, I'm so relieved!" Emily smiled. "Thank you for letting me know! So, they decided to do the surgery after all?"

As if giving a report, Grant explained, "The dog had surgery, and the vet was able to stop the internal bleeding. Last I heard, they thought he would make a full recovery."

Though relieved, Grant's report didn't quite satisfy her. For some reason, he didn't seem to want to talk much about it. He was giving short, precise answers, and Emily wanted the details.

"But who paid for the surgery?" she couldn't stop herself from asking. "The younger man didn't seem to be willing to pay, and I hate the thought of the older man trying to pay for something I doubt he could afford. And he could hardly hear well enough to understand what was happening. The vet said the surgery could cost several thousand dollars, and the dog could still die."

"I paid for it."

Emily stopped breathing. Her eyes locked with Grant's, and she felt as if she were searching his soul. She saw the truth in their depths, and it left her feeling shocked and in awe. "You paid for it?" she clarified, still having trouble wrapping her mind around such a selfless act.

Grant simply nodded again briefly.

Emily swallowed and smiled up at Grant. It was a smile that started at her toes and seemed to extend a pure, exciting joy all the way up to her eyes. "Shall we go have coffee, Mr. Dillon?"

Chapter Seventeen

"FIRST, I need to apologize," Grant said, wasting no time after they got their coffee and sat down at a table in a corner. He set the notebook down between them and looked at her steadily. "I read your notebook."

"Ok," Emily said, thinking that didn't sound too horrible. It wasn't as if she had a lock on the thing.

Undeterred, Grant continued, "When I first found it at the vet clinic, I started looking through it to see if there was a name, phone number, or just a clue that would help me find you. I saw the poem you wrote near the beginning, and I thought it was beautiful. I've since read the whole notebook multiple times, and I have to tell you that your words have really made me think and change my perspective on how I interact with others."

Emily self-consciously looked around the small coffee shop. They were seated at a corner table in comfy chairs with a table between them that overlooked the street. The evening crowd wasn't a big one. Though the street outside bustled with a steady stream of pedestrians getting off work for the day, the few patrons inside seemed to pick up their coffee only to return to join the stream outside. Very few people sat soaking in the warmth and soothing atmosphere of browns and greens mixed with warm, old brick walls and furniture that begged to be occupied.

Though his words reached her ears only, the knowledge that he'd read her personal thoughts embarrassed her enough to keep her eyes on her coffee cup even as she tried to minimize their importance. "Mr. Dillon, I don't mind that you read it. I write things in notebooks just to get my thoughts down. It helps me think. A lot of times, I just write to-do lists. Sometimes I just write random thoughts or things I'm working through. Although I didn't intend for my personal thoughts to be read by strangers, it really touches me to know that they had an impact on you."

"Please call me Grant," he said.

Even if his words hadn't been so personal, Grant Dillon's good looks would have been enough to keep her eyes averted, trying not to notice his honest, soul-searching blue eyes, his dark hair that waved away from his face at just the right angle, and the scruffy five-o'clock shadow that only added to his handsome intrigue.

"And I'm Emily," she replied back, her voice tight.

"Emily, I don't think you fully understand what I mean," he said hesitantly, idly stirring his coffee more than it actually needed. "Your words and thoughts are more than just casual. They have beauty and meaning that can change people. I know because they changed me. Because of what I read, I didn't walk away from my daughter when I normally would have. I spent the time to figure out what was bothering her, and our relationship is better because of it. I also stopped and tried to help two people who'd been in a fender bender. I earned a punch to the jaw for it, but I also prevented a little boy from watching his dad participate in a traumatic brawl."

"You were punched?" Emily gasped, immediately inspecting his strong jaw for injury.

Grant shrugged. "It was worth it for that little boy. He and my daughter are only two examples of people who have been helped through the inspiration of your words. I have others to tell you. Even my daughter took your words to heart to make a difference and not walk away. However, what I really want to know is your story. While reading your notebook, I couldn't help but wonder about your personal reason behind the words. It was obvious that something prompted your thoughts. What was it? What made you want to help those on the sidelines of life?"

Emily read respect in his eyes. He thought she was special. He thought she was a hero, maybe even a shining paradigm who helps the poor and brokenhearted. Clearly, he admired her, which made her feel like a complete fraud. She didn't deserve his admiration, and the sooner he understood what kind of person she really was, the better.

Emily took a sip of her still-scalding coffee and pushed ahead through the discomfort. "I'm really sorry to disappoint you, Grant, but I fear there has been a misunderstanding. I am not a role model. I am not some kind-hearted saint who dedicates her life to others. I wrote the poem and everything else in the notebook because I messed up. And my mistake was so bad that I hurt someone. Someone was physically injured because of my actions."

"What happened?" Grant asked, watching her steadily without flinching.

Part of her wanted to shock him. He needed to know the kind of person she was. He needed to know that in this story, she wasn't the hero, she was the villain.

So she told him flatly, with no hesitation and no excuses. "I turned left on a flashing yellow light. It wasn't intentional. I thought the light was green, and it wasn't. By the time I realized it, a car struck me. The other driver was injured. The last I heard, she shattered her foot, and there may have been other issues. It was my fault. I was the one who failed to yield."

Emily waited for him to respond. She figured he would probably jump to her defense and try to assure her that it really was just an accident. But she'd heard it all multiple times before. She didn't want his sympathy; she didn't deserve it.

However, instead of what she expected him to say, he asked, "How does the poem fit in with the accident? Are you now trying to earn atonement through good deeds?"

"No, not at all," Emily answered, surprised at his theory. First, he'd assumed her to be the hero, and now he was misunderstanding what she was trying to say. "I honestly just told you that part to demonstrate the truth that I'm not a person worth admiring."

Pausing and taking a deep breath, she continued. "After the accident, the police and ambulance arrived. They took the other driver away and cleaned everything up. A police officer wrote me a 'failure to yield' ticket, and two trucks came and took both vehicles away. After the mess was cleaned up as if it had never happened, I sat on the corner and waited for my mom to come pick me up since I had no other way home. While waiting, I sat there crying while people came and went at the busy intersection. Not a single person stopped and asked what was wrong or if I was okay. No one even spared a glance my direction. It was as if I wasn't even there. It was a horrible, lonely feeling, and it was that which I longed to prevent when I wrote that poem. It made me wonder how many people I passed every day, not seeing their needs, and I didn't want anyone else to ever feel the way I did in that moment."

She looked back up into Grant's eyes, but when she couldn't read his expression, she looked away in embarrassment. Even though she had spilled the truth in all its shame, she still spoke bravely, though no longer able to hold his gaze steady.

She swallowed, feeling the silence stretch until she could no longer take it. "I'm sorry to disillusion you so, Grant. I know that story is probably not at all what you expected. Unfortunately, I am not a character worth admiring, and the reason for the poem is simple and rather mundane, not at all a big epic with great-life changing meaning for those who read my beat-up little notebook. It's just about me crying on a street corner because I'd done something wrong and hoping that I can catch someone else's tears the next time I see my place on the curb occupied."

Grant's hand touched hers where it rested on the table. Then he gently enfolded it in his.

Emily's heart leaped at the contact, and her gaze scrambled back up to his.

"Emily Jansen, I truly think you may be the most amazing woman I have ever met." His voice was husky with sincerity. "I don't admire you because I think you're perfect, but because you are flawed and imperfect. You let God shine through all of your struggles and mistakes, blessing others because of it. Sometimes the simplest things are the most profound. Your words, and the pain that it took to write them, show in every stroke of your pen. I am sad that you went through that experience of the accident, and I hurt for both your pain and that of the other driver, but Emily, look around you. God used it to make something beautiful."

Emily shook her head. "You talk about it like it was in the past tense, but it isn't. It's today. It's every moment that I know I hurt someone. It's an ever-present cloud suffocating me because I know I could lose everything I have. It's only been six months, and the case isn't anywhere near settled. I don't understand how you can call this good when there is no happily ever after in sight."

"You can't always neatly classify things into good and bad," Grant replied thoughtfully. "Sometimes they're both. It was bad that you got in an accident and someone was hurt, but God doesn't necessarily work on our timetable. While you might not feel ready to see the good or stop punishing yourself for a mistake, that doesn't mean that God is unable to use you and your experience to help others and show His love today."

"I think you overstate the influence of a little poem," Emily said skeptically. He was just trying to make her feel better. He'd read and liked her notebook. That really did mean a lot, but there was no sense in exaggerating. If she worked on it, she might even be able to accept the idea that God had used her notebook to touch this reporter. But reaching for anything beyond that was unrealistic and unnecessary.

"Emily, I knew you were someone I wanted to know even before I read your notebook. When you prayed for those two men and that dog, I can't tell you how in awe I was. I didn't know how a young woman could be so brave and loving toward complete strangers. Then I read your notebook, and right there in black and white, it explained why you had done it. But I wasn't the only one who connected to you and your words. That night after I almost walked away from my 14-year old daughter, she asked me why I'd stopped. I told her the whole story of you. She also related to you and your words. Sitting on a street corner is how she felt after her mom died. In turn, your words and truth inspired her to help another girl at school. It isn't just me. Emily, this is a whole lot bigger than you realize."

Emily swallowed with difficulty. Grant was telling her things she didn't want to hear, and it wasn't just his words that were communicating. His eyes said that his admiration for her had only grown. There was no denying the electricity that sparked with the contact of their hands. She couldn't deny the physical attraction, but there was also a deeper connection. Unfortunately, it was one she couldn't risk exploring. The sooner Grant knew that, the better. Maybe if he knew there was no chance of them being romantically involved, then he wouldn't be so insistent about the impact of her words.

With her goal of being blunt and ripping off the bandage quickly, Emily explained, "Grant, I'm not someone you should want to be involved with. In fact, every man should stay clear of me. I'm messed up. I have more issues than even I want to deal with, and I certainly wouldn't want someone else chained to them. The accident left me with severe anxiety. I practically have a panic attack every time I drive. I have flashbacks. I am not well, and most days I barely manage to function. Besides that, the insurance case for the accident still isn't closed and likely won't be for a year and a half. The other driver has two years to file suit against me. I'm even concerned about my parents because, while I'm just a teacher and don't have much money, my dad's name is on my car with mine. If someone was desperate enough, they could sue my parents as well!"

Grant looked confused. "So, is your plan just to stop living and keep everyone who might care about you at arm's length until you know for sure that you're safe and not going to get sued?"

Emily shrugged. "It's been working so far."

With his forehead still wrinkled in confusion, he persisted, "What you're saying is that you are simply not going to allow God to bring anything or anyone good into your life until the matter of your accident is resolved."

While those might not be the exact words she'd choose to use…

Before she could respond, he continued. "And the reason is because you can't trust that God will take care of you. You can't trust that you'll be okay if you do get sued or don't. You can't trust that He may have some good purpose for you that is beyond the accident."

Grant paused, clearly looking at her earnestly to make sure she was listening. "Emily have you ever considered that what you may see as a huge barricade, God may see as something so small that He intends to use it for you to step your foot on while getting to the destination? What if the big deal isn't what happened or what will happen, but is what God intends to use you for through it?"

Emily looked at him, dumbstruck. It seemed strange that she had just met this man, and yet they were holding deep spiritual discussions that even bordered on arguments! He very passionately spoke his opinion as if both it and she mattered very much to him. What seemed almost stranger, though, was the realization that it didn't *feel* strange that they should be talking like this. It was almost as if they already knew each other on a level of connection deeper than any Emily could recall feeling before.

Emily blinked, not sure how to respond. She couldn't seem to process even a little of what he'd said. She knew it was similar to some of the same things her parents had tried to tell her. But somehow, it was completely different coming from him. What he said made perfect sense, but yet again, knowing something and doing something were two entirely different things. It was the doing part that she just didn't think she could do.

"I don't—"

"There you are!" A woman with dark hair rushed up to their table. "Grant, you found her! When I got back from my meeting, they told me at the office that you had found her. I bribed Wendy to tell me where she thought you'd gone. I just had to see for myself!"

Grant's eyes were alarmed, "Susan, I don't think—"

"Wait a minute," Emily said. "You look really familiar." Quickly, she glanced from the top of her dark hair, to the nicely tailored business suit, to the red heels that clicked every time she stepped.

Emily's eyes flew wide. "You're the woman from the store Saturday night! My bags broke in the parking lot when it was dark and snowy. You helped me pick things up and gave me your canvas bags!"

Susan put her hand to her mouth. "That was you! To think we had been looking all over for you, and I ran into you in the parking lot of some random store!"

"Wait a minute, Susan, you stopped and helped someone? In the dark? And the snow?" Grant was incredulous.

"You said you almost walked away," Emily mused, her

thoughts tumbling over each other as she tried to sort everything out.

Susan looked both bashful and slightly defensive, which made for an interesting sight. "Grant, you act like I've never helped another human being in my life." There was the defensive "I read the poem, too, you know. You showed it to me. I'm not entirely without a heart. I thought about it." There was the bashful.

Grant grinned from ear to ear, clearly pleased that Emily's words had made an impact even on Susan. "Susan is my boss at the newspaper," Grant explained. "She is not very soft and fluffy, so hearing that she'd gone out of her way to help someone is pretty much a Christmas miracle!"

Susan haughtily lifted her head as if finished discussing her personal thoughts and actions. Snagging a nearby chair, she brought it forward with a screech of its metal legs and sat in between Grant and Emily. Turning to Emily, she beamed, "Now you see how important it is for us to make plans. If your notebook can touch and change me, then think how much good it will do when the whole world reads Grant's story about you!"

Grant held up his hand, "Ummm... Susan, can we talk about this later? I don't think this is—

"Story?" Emily's gaze swung to Grant's. "You're writing a story about me?"

"Of course, he is!" Susan gushed enthusiastically. "The notebook needs to be shared! That's why he's been searching for you. He has the story pretty much written, but he needed to know your story to finish it. Did you get it, Grant? I need the final copy tonight."

"That's what this is all about?" Emily gasped, her mouth completely dry. "You're writing a story about me for your newspaper? That's why you needed to find me?"

"No, Emily. It isn't like that," Grant protested.

"Of course, it is!" Susan inserted helpfully. "We couldn't

actually publish your writing without your permission. We didn't have confirmation that you were the one who'd written it in the first place. Now that we have everything, this story is going to be big! I'm talking interviews and appearances on every network and every morning and late show between now and Christmas!"

"No," Emily said simply and firmly. With great deliberation, she placed her napkin beside her half cup of coffee, stood up, and grabbed her purse. "I'm sorry I misunderstood, Mr. Dillon. I didn't realize this was an interview for your article. If I had known, I could have saved you a lot of time."

With jaw firm and eyes unblinking, she said clearly, "I do not give you permission to use my writing."

Reaching down, she grabbed her notebook off the table and held it to her chest protectively. "You do not have permission to mention me, my name, or anything about me."

Grant stood and reached out his hands, trying to calm her. "Please, Emily, just let me explain."

"You have already explained more than enough. And I've explained as well." Lowering her voice, she whispered brokenly, "I told you about the accident and how there is an open case still against me. If I'm suddenly all over the news, how will that look? It would be like putting a target directly on me! There is no way I could risk something like that!"

"I'm sure we can work something out," Susan said, her tone patronizing.

"No, we can't," Emily snapped. "Let me be clear. You may not write an article about me or use my writing in any way. Nor may you look for me or contact me in any way."

Holding clear eye contact with both Grant and Susan, she spoke, a hard edge to her voice that left no slack as far as to her meaning. "Leave me alone."

Then she turned and ran out the door.

Chapter Eighteen

EMILY felt like she didn't breathe until she pulled into her own garage forty-five minutes later. Then she shut off her car engine, lowered the garage door, turned off the headlights, and cried.

How could one evening be one of the best and worst at the exact same time?

She finally opened the car door and got out. Completely numb, she made it inside her small house. She opened the refrigerator door, thinking that she should eat something. But she couldn't. She thought about calling her mom, but she already knew what her parents would say. She didn't want to hear it.

Instead, she shut the door, sat cross-legged on the linoleum floor, and wept again.

She had so wanted to believe Grant. She had been skeptical about all of his talk of how her poem and the rest of her writing had made a difference in his own life and the lives of others. But she had wanted to believe him.

Despite her objections, a big part of her wanted to grasp onto the hope that he offered—the hope that said that she wasn't serving a sentence, and God wasn't waiting to do good things with her. He was doing them now.

It was as if offered a flicker of light in a pitch-black cave. Maybe God wasn't wasting her pain. Even though the ugliness had been her own fault, maybe God could change her to be more like Him and use her experience to help others. If all that had been true, wouldn't that have made her trauma more bearable? Instead of a senseless mistake that haunted her, she could have given it all to Him with the reassurance and hope that He could redeem it.

But that had all been a lie. Just like that light, her hope had been snuffed out.

Or had it?

Grant seemed so genuine. The way he looked at her made her heart flutter. It was as if he saw something in her that nobody else did, yet when he looked into her eyes, it felt as if he saw to the deepest part of her soul. Maybe he just saw what nobody else had ever looked for. Even with knowing everything she was and everything she'd done, he'd still held that gaze steadily without flinching. Her story hadn't scared him. He hadn't been shocked or appalled that she had been at fault in an accident and hurt someone. He hadn't even seemed put-off about her anxiety or the fact that she had a potential lawsuit hanging over her head. Instead of stepping away, it was as if, knowing all of that, he'd still deliberately taken a step closer.

What if he hadn't been lying? He'd openly said that he thought her words were powerful enough to change people. Even before Susan had shown up, it was as if he were hinting at doing an article. It made sense now.

Did wanting to write a story on her automatically qualify him as dishonest?

She had been shocked by Susan's interruption. It was clear Grant did not want Emily told the way Susan had handled things. What if his purpose really had been just what he said the whole time? He'd said her words and story had inspired him, and it sure seemed like he longed to share that inspiration with others. If his goal really was to inspire others to see those sitting and crying on the street corner, wasn't that a noble goal? One that she should do everything she could to support?

She couldn't let him write a story about her, but she could at least be kind and supportive, that is if he really was a decent guy who was telling the truth.

Emily stood and stretched her muscles out from their cramped position. Then she grabbed her phone and a tin of Christmas cookies one of her students had given her and curled up on her couch. She brought up the internet on her phone and did a search for Grant Dillon at *The Brighton Daily*.

Feeling a little bit like a stalker, she read his bio and everything she could find about him. She learned where he went to high school and college, when he'd gotten married, when his daughter had been born, and when his wife had passed away after a two-year battle with aggressive breast cancer.

She looked him up on Facebook, but saw he had all of his privacy settings current on his personal page. She couldn't access anything other than his profile picture, and she didn't have the guts to push the "add a friend" button.

She then turned to reading some of the articles he had written. Though she had read articles by him before, she hadn't paid attention to the who behind the well-written story. Now it was more personal, and it soon became very clear that Grant was a gifted journalist. It seemed he could write on any subject and still communicate something touching and profound.

Seeing his most recent article, one that had just been released today, Emily clicked on it. The title grabbed her immediately. There was something about, "What They Remember," that piqued her curiosity. Then she began to read:

Many didn't realize that an important event happened this weekend at Sunset Memory Care and Assisted Living here in Brighton Falls. Here are five people who were at the event—five people who remember and five you should remember, too:

Chelsey Simmons:

Miss Simmons is a second-grade teacher at a local school. She recently had the difficult task of moving her mom to a memory care facility. While Chelsey had been her mother's sole caregiver for a long time, Alzheimer's disease reached the point that safety necessitated that Chelsey seek full-time care for the woman who had once cared for her.

Chelsey visits her mother at Sunset every day, and she has been struck by the observation that not many of the residents have visitors.

So, she remembered those who are often forgotten.

She remembered that even though many of the residents can't remember names or even people, they can remember what joy feels like. They know the feeling of being loved, and they can tell when someone cares.

Chelsey organized Saturday's event to remember those who no longer can remember. She brought children to sing and deliver presents to the residents. They decorated a huge tree, entertained, and brought smiles to those who needed them. Though the residents of Sunset won't remember her name or maybe even what happened at the party, they will know the joy of a moment.

Max Fredericks:

Max is a 5-year old kindergarten boy who attended the Sunset party with his mom and his music teacher. He sang Christmas songs, helped some of the residents unwrap Christmas gift ornaments to hang on the tree, and brought joy wherever his feet landed and his smile flashed. Max will remember when he was a superhero. An elderly resident named Pamela loaned him a (lap blanket) cape, and he flew around the room to the ooh's and ahhs of his captive audience. Most of all, Max will remember making the residents smile.

Henry Garinger:

Henry isn't a resident at Sunset, but his wife, Pamela, is. Other than Chelsey Simmons, Henry is the only daily visitor. When Henry isn't visiting Pamela, he's home alone with his dog as his only company. Pamela and Henry had two children, one of which has long passed away. The other lives out of state.

Henry remembers a lot.

He remembers the first time he kissed Pamela on the porch of her parents' house.

He remembers when he got on one knee and asked her to marry him.

He remembers the scent of honeysuckle on their wedding day.

He remembers the feel of holding his newborn daughter in his arms.

He remembers countless joys and many tears.

Jobs lost and gained, houses bought and sold, fights, vacations, camping trips, ball games, board games, laughing so hard he cried.

And the marks on the wall that told the passage of time.

He remembers Christmas.

He remembers the day he brought Pamela to Sunset, and the first night he couldn't sleep beside her.

He remembers that she doesn't always remember him.

So he remembers for her.

Pamela Garinger:

Some days Pamela remembers lots of things, some days she doesn't. But there are a few things she never forgets:

The feel of Henry's hand in hers as they sit close on the couch.

Knowing that Henry loves her (even though she sometimes doesn't know who he is).

The knowledge that they belong together. He is hers, and she is his.

How to smile.

The comfort of Henry's presence.

Joy.

The 5th person on the party list is you.

What will you remember this Christmas?

Emily sucked in a breath and tried to stop her tears. She hadn't known she physically could cry anymore, and yet there she was, trying to finish reading Grant's article through wet, blurry eyes.

There was absolutely no doubt that every word Grant had spoken to her was true. His article was touching and echoed in her own writing in so many ways. A deep part of her longed for Grant to use her words for inspiration and write a message that beautiful.

She stood to her feet, running her hands through her hair and pacing.

As much as she wanted to, she couldn't do it.

Lord, I can't do it. It would be stupid. If the wrong people hear about it, maybe they'll think that I'm trying to use the accident for my own gain. If Susan is right and I suddenly become so popular that I need to start doing interviews, people will see me and assume I'm getting paid and have lots of money. They will think that I'm trying to use someone else's misfortune for my financial gain.

Ok, Lord, please help me get this off my mind. I'm not going to let Grant use my writing. I'm not. There is no reason when you look at all the problems and complications that could happen. There's no reason at all.

Except if I want you to.

The thought caught her off guard.

You wouldn't want me to do that, Lord. You already know how I struggle with anxiety and how I've just been waiting every day for this nightmare to be over. I can do it after the case closes. That will work. Maybe next Christmas Grant will still want to do the article.

Not next year. Now.

Emily took a deep breath, trying to steady herself. It wasn't as if an audible voice were speaking to her, but every excuse she put up had a very insistent thought that was the exact opposite immediately following it.

Finally, out of frustration, she threw her hands up and cried aloud to God. "I don't know what you want me to do! Am I supposed to just give it all up? Am I supposed to throw caution to the wind and trust that You will be there for me, even when it seems like a really foolish thing to do? I just can't do it, Lord! Please don't ask me to!"

Why?

"Because I'm afraid!" The cry came out in a sob, and with it came release.

She was afraid. All of her excuses had come down to one—fear.

With that realization came another one close on its heels: Fear was not an excuse God would accept.

I have not given you a spirit of fear

Be strong and courageous

Fear not, for I am with you

The Bible was full of verse after verse proclaiming that she need not fear. If God was who He said He was, fear had no room when compared to the creator and commander of the universe.

Still hiccupping sobs, her gaze collided with the notebook sitting on the counter where she'd left it.

Desperately, she reached for it, trying for one last escape plan. Maybe she was blowing things out of proportion. Her writing likely wasn't as good as Grant had insinuated. He'd move on to a different story, and she could just let it all go if she could just verify that there was nothing special in the notebook. Then she wouldn't need to worry about being afraid if this was all unnecessary.

Give me eyes to see what isn't shown,

Ears to hear what isn't said,

Hands to do what You want,

And the courage to not walk away.

She felt slightly nauseated as her own words convicted her.

She knew right then that if she walked away from this opportunity, then she would be, in essence, leaving herself and many others on that street corner with no one to care. If her words could inspire others to realize the same revelation, looking to see those who get passed by every day, then that's what she should do. Even if it cost her, she couldn't in good conscience walk away from those who others may not see sitting there.

"Help me, Lord. This isn't going to be easy."

She swallowed with difficulty and picked up the business card that had fallen from her notebook when she had opened it. Then she picked up her phone and carefully dialed the number on the card.

"Don't let me walk away," she whispered desperately.

The line answered. "Hello?"

It sounded almost like the voice or a child—a little girl.

Emily drew the phone away from her head and looked at the number.

"Hello?" the voice asked again, still young.

"Hi," Emily answered, jumping in abruptly. "I was looking for Grant Dillon. Did I get the wrong number?"

"Oh, no. I'm Grant's daughter, Mila. He's just... busy right now. Can I take a message?"

"Sure, I guess so. I'm Emily Jan—"

"You're Emily?" the voice hissed incredulously.

"Yes," Emily replied cautiously.

"I can't believe it's really you! My dad is talking to his boss about you right now! Susan actually came here to our house, and she and Dad are arguing about you in his office! I just borrowed Dad's phone earlier to text Alexis's mom's phone. And that reminds me, I really need to thank you."

Emily shook her head, trying to keep up with Mila's pace and fluid conversational subjects. "Why do you need to thank me?" she managed.

"Dad let me read your notebook, and it really got me thinking. I thought about all the times that I'd wished someone had noticed how I felt, and I didn't want anyone else to feel that way. The next day, I saw a girl from class who always sits alone at lunch. Instead of walking past and sitting with my friends, I had lunch with her. At first, I was pretty embarrassed and thought I'd completely failed when she didn't even say two words to me. Now I think she was just so shocked, she didn't know what to do. We've been talking a lot, and she's a really good friend. If I hadn't stopped like your notebook said, I would have never found out what a great person Alexis is, and she would have kept sitting alone with no one noticing."

Emily's throat constricted. Grant was right, and Mila's words just confirmed she was doing the right thing. With sharing her notebook, she could extend help to so many people who needed someone to notice. Even if she got sued and lost everything, Emily thought that by God's standard, she would have gained much more than she lost.

"Thank you for telling me, Mila," Emily said warmly. "It means a lot to me."

"You're welcome," Mila said. "I guess you'd like to talk to my dad."

"Yes, I would. I really need to talk to him right away."

"I can try to interrupt him, but he and Susan are really arguing. Susan wants Dad to write that story about you, but he is refusing. I think he might actually get fired!"

Oh, no! Grant can't get fired because of me!

"Mila, hand the phone to your dad," Emily said firmly. "Interrupt him if you have to. Tell him it's me, and I need to talk to him."

"Ok," Mila whispered. "I'll try!"

Emily heard Mila scurry over to a door and open it. Suddenly, the voices Emily had heard in the background got much louder.

"Susan, I already wrote you a story. It was the one about the assisted living party, and it was just released today. I told you when I turned it in that I wasn't going to write the other one."

"And I said you didn't have a choice," Susan hissed. "That story was good. The response from it has been great, but you and I both know that story is only a small part of the larger story about Emily. Now, you will do that story. I will talk to our lawyers to make sure we have our bases covered. You don't have to quote her writing, just give the gist."

"No, I will not write anything to do with Emily. Fire me if you must, but she did not give her permission. I will not violate that for anything you may say or do."

"Need I remind you that you have a contract, Mr. Dillon? If you refuse to write this article, I will hold you in breach of contract, and then I will fire you. Do you under—"

"Dad!" Mila's voice shouted.

Into the sudden silence, Mila continued calmly, "Dad, Emily wants to talk to you."

Emily actually heard Susan's gasp.

Then she heard Grant's voice, but he wasn't speaking to her. "Susan, I'd like to take this call privately. I'm sure Mila can get you something to drink in the kitchen."

Though Emily thought some grumbling was involved, she heard the door click shut behind Susan, and Grant's voice immediately came through the line.

"Emily? Are you there?"

"Yes, Grant, it's me," she replied.

Then, with a deep breath, she said firmly. "Grant, use my poem, my notebook, my name, anything you need. You have my full permission. Just write the story."

Chapter Nineteen

"**THAT** was the last paper for you to sign!" Susan said perkily. "You're all done!"

She cleared everything off the desk except a *Brighton Daily* pen, which she generously bestowed on Emily.

"Thank you so much for coming by to take care of those things," Susan said sweetly. "I know it was a long drive, especially since you had to make it after work."

Emily simply nodded. "You're sure there's nothing else I need to do?" Emily clarified. She really didn't want to get home to find out she needed to make another trip tomorrow.

"No, I think we've made all the arrangements," she said sorting through the papers. "Well, Grant made the arrangements, but we followed through. We consulted with your lawyer, so everything should be fine on that angle. Grant insisted we pay for the consult as well, so that's taken care of. Wendy should have your check at the front desk. It's just the standard fee to use your poem. It's not much—probably just enough to buy your mom a Christmas present. You retain all rights to your poem, of course. Since that's the only one Grant quoted in his story, then you should be set."

"What about interviews? You said I wouldn't need to do interviews, right?" Emily said with clear anxiety.

"Right. Grant is running the media circuit. Since the article came out this morning, he's already busy with his phone ringing nonstop to schedule interviews, but he seems to think he'll be able to handle those. Technically, the papers should have been signed earlier, before the story was released, but the lawyer said as long as you signed by the end of the day, it should be fine."

"You're sure I'm not going to be hounded?" Emily said skeptically. Wouldn't some of Grant's sudden popularity inevitably spill over to her?

"Have you read the article, Emily?" Susan asked, openly curious.

"No, I haven't," Emily replied honestly. "I haven't had a chance. I taught all day and then came straight here after work."

Susan smiled. "I'm sure Grant would want to show you himself, but why don't I get you some copies before you leave? Let me just say that Grant did a fantastic job. I think you will be very well pleased with how he communicated your story while also maintaining your privacy. Mark my words, this one is going to earn him some awards."

"Where is Grant?" Emily said, attempting to be casual. She had thought she'd see him when she came to sign Susan's papers, but now she was done and still hadn't seen him at all. "I was hoping to run into him before I left."

Susan smiled knowingly. "I don't even know where he is. When I said he was running, I meant that literally. I saw him run past once today. Mostly he's been talking and making arrangements with the big bosses, shows, and networks. The story went viral within the first hour we released it this morning."

Emily nodded and stood. It certainly didn't sound like she'd be able to see Grant anytime soon, so there was no use in waiting around. If she headed home now, she could at least leave the city before it got completely dark.

"Why don't I tell Grant I saw you? I'm sure he'll give you a call as soon as he can. You know, I think all our copies here are already gone," Susan said, lifting up a few stacks of paper. "All of the other employees must have swiped them. Why don't you head down and get some from Wendy at the front desk? She'll have some, and you need to stop by there before 5:00 to pick up your check anyway."

After thanking Susan, she hurried to the front lobby. Susan's papers had only taken a few minutes, but she didn't want Wendy to leave early without giving Emily what she needed.

Reaching the front desk, Wendy smiled and handed Emily the check without her even needing to ask.

"Ummm..." Emily hesitated, not exactly sure how to ask. "Susan mentioned that you might have some extra copies of today's paper. I was wondering if I could have a couple?"

"Oh, my goodness!" Wendy's eyes flew wide. "You don't have any yet? Let me find you some." She turned around and began rummaging through the counter area.

"Don't worry about it, Wendy. I already ordered her a box." Grant's deep voice from right behind her shoulder sent a shiver all the way through her.

"Oh, good!" Wendy sighed in relief. "We've had so many people come in for copies today that we've had to order more. It just wouldn't have been right for Emily not to have some."

"Hi," Emily said shyly, not sure what to say now that Grant was actually here.

"Hi," he smiled back. "I see you're getting ready to leave. Do you care if I borrow you for a few minutes?"

"Sure," Emily said, turning to walk with him toward the front door.

"Oh, Emily?" Wendy called from behind the counter.

Emily turned.

The receptionist smiled, her eyes twinkling. "I wanted to thank you for the shoes." Then more seriously, she continued. "I will definitely be putting them to good use. I don't think I'll look at people the same way ever again."

Emily shook her head, not understanding.

"I'll explain," Grant said quietly, a trace of humor threading his voice.

They didn't make it to the front door, but instead, Grant took her elbow and led her to the corner between the front window and the elevator. There weren't any seats, but Grant pushed a newspaper into her hands. "Read it," he instructed quietly. "It's going to be warmer in here than outside, and I don't want to wait."

Emily looked up at him in amusement. His excitement was obvious and reminded her of a little boy who couldn't wait to show off a masterpiece he'd just drawn.

Emily obediently opened the paper and quickly found the story by Grant Dillon.

"A Cinderella Christmas," she read, thinking that a curious title.

Then, with the newspaper lobby still bustling and the elevators dinging intermittently, Emily read Grant's story.

It was like nothing she'd read before but was almost a combination between a mystery and a fairy tale. The opening was a description of the scene at the Vets and Pets Specialty Hospital. Grant described it perfectly, somehow instilling all the emotions of the moment into the words on the page. From there, the story launched into his search for who his boss had termed "his Cinderella." The tale followed Grant's perspective from his shock and admiration of her at the vet clinic, to his awe at discovering the poem in her notebook, to each of the instances where he tried to put her words into practice. He recounted how he stopped and talked to his daughter, how he got punched for trying to help someone, and even how he fixed his boss's squeaky chair. The common thread through each instance was his search for Cinderella.

Finally, when he was covering a party at Sunset Memory Care and Assisted Living, he had an epiphany. When seeing a child bringing joy to an elderly couple, he realized that he had already found Cinderella. Though he may not ever find *his* Cinderella, he had found that others could live out her message and help those who are normally overlooked. With his newfound peace, he went to interview the woman in charge of the party.

Emily gasped, her eyes darting down the page, then back up to read it again.

"Grant, did this really happen?" she asked, shocked at the twist. "I was at the party at Sunset. I didn't notice you, and I certainly had no idea any of this was going on!"

Grant paled slightly. "That was you? I thought I saw you, but then when I tried to chase you down, you disappeared. I thought I was just so desperate to find you that I imagined someone else looked like you."

"You must have seen me as I was leaving," Emily explained. "I didn't stay long after giving Chelsey the cards and gifts from my class. I wanted to get back home before it was too late. I certainly would have stayed had I known this was going on! It seems like an unbelievable coincidence, with a strong dose of the miraculous!"

Grant grinned. "Yes! It really did happen! After talking to Henry and Pamela Garinger, I spoke again with Chelsey, who told me that she got the idea of helping those we normally overlook from watching a boy stand up for another boy at recess. Apparently, the boy said he did it because of what he'd overheard his parents discussing the night before. The boy's mother was a friend of Chelsey's and was already at the party helping, so of course, I asked her about it."

"And she said her husband saw a guy get punched for trying to help two drivers who had been in an accident?" Emily asked incredulously.

"Yes!" Grant insisted gleefully. "That's what happened! A woman named Brandi talked about how impressed her husband had been with how the man 'didn't walk away!'"

Emily shook her head. "That's mind-boggling! I can't quite wrap my mind around it!"

"If you think about it, Emily, we don't know who is affected when we help others. This was just one thread. But it's like a web, and we don't know how far and wide the message of your poem spread, even before I wrote that story. There's no way of knowing for sure, but thankfully, God has given us the evidence to know that people heard, responded, and acted on the message already. He blessed us by revealing one strand. Can you imagine what it will look like when people put your poem in action and help people, who then, in turn, do the same thing and help more people? Emily, it will extend to an exponentially expanding web where nobody walks away!"

Emily was so bombarded with emotion that the paper in her hand shook. "Here, let me finish," she said, drawing her gaze back to the paper. "I'm almost done."

It wasn't a short article, but Grant had blended a reporting style with that of storytelling to create something that was succinct yet communicated a heft of emotion. Though he had used her poem as inspiration, it wasn't really her story at all, it was his. The reader felt what Grant did and rooted for him to find Cinderella. And just when they thought that he had given up and come to terms with the message instead of the person, a twist resurrected the hope in anyone who read. It was so much so that, even though she knew what happened next, she found herself longing to pray with Grant Dillan that he would find her.

Reaching the very last two paragraphs of the article, Emily read Grant's words slowly and carefully.

Just when I thought I'd never find the woman who didn't walk away, she walked into my office the day of my deadline, looking for her notebook.

I found my Cinderella, and she is much more than I ever imagined those long nights of looking and praying for her.

But what I learned most from this experience is that Cinderella's words are universal—Cinderella's shoes fit everyone. This Christmas, make sure you use them.

Don't walk away.

Something that sounded very near to a sob escaped from her throat, and Emily clasped her hand over her mouth. He had managed everything so perfectly, delivering the message of her poem better than she could have dreamed. And he did it all while protecting her privacy and not revealing anything about her.

"Emily, are you okay?" Grant asked, concerned to see tears streaming freely down her face.

Emily smiled and nodded, trying to gain control. "I'm okay." For the first time in a long time, she really meant it. She really was okay.

Whether she got sued or didn't get sued.

Whether Grant was the one God planned for her, or he decided he didn't like her so much after he got to know her more.

Whatever came her way tomorrow…

She was okay.

Grant's article had shown her that God's plans were better than hers, and she could trust Him to use even the ugliest part of her life. Yes, she was still scared, but even if the worst happened, she knew God would be there ready to make something out of the most difficult circumstances. She knew that she may not get to always see God's purpose, but because she had seen this one, she knew she could trust God for all of those she couldn't see.

"Grant, it's beautiful," she said. Looking into his warm, sparkling eyes, she felt something stir, and she was overwhelmed with the wonder that this man already seemed at least half in love with her. Maybe that was how it should be. He'd fallen for her words—the essence of who she was and the confession of her soul.

With each breath she took, she was falling hard for the man who had paid for the surgery for someone else's dog and who'd had the courage to put her words in action.

Grant glanced at his watch. "Do you feel like taking a walk for a few minutes? I have some time before they start looking for me."

"Yes, Grant, I'd love to take a walk with you."

They exited the building and hurried down the steps. When they got a few yards away from the office, their gait slowed.

The sky was relinquishing its last bits of light, and the streetlights were blinking on overhead. It had been snowing off and on all day, leaving the trees and every surface laden with fresh snow. The smell of coffee wafted from the coffee shop across the street, even at this hour, and Emily caught the faint aroma of gingerbread, though she didn't know from where it came.

Emily walked silently, watching the city yet wrapped up with thoughts of Grant's story and the intricacy with which God had worked. However, she was also very aware of the masculine man beside her. Though her thoughts tumbled with numerous comments and remarks on his story, she was suddenly overcome with shyness and couldn't even make herself comment on the mysterious gingerbread aroma.

Maybe she was reading too much into his article. Maybe she really wasn't his Cinderella but had only been a muse for a project for work. Even now, maybe he was just wasting a few minutes before jetting off for his round of late interviews.

Then she felt the warmth of his hand steal over hers. Emily's heart fluttered, and the only coherent thought she could manage was that she never wanted him to let go.

They passed a few others on the street. People shopping or hurrying home after work. Some were just looking up from reading an article on their phones, while others were coming out from their houses after watching coverage of a viral story that was chasing Christmas in terms of popularity. A few others had been shown random kindness in the bustle of the crazy Christmas season.

They didn't know the couple they passed on the street, and in two weeks' time, they probably wouldn't remember the exact words that had so touched them or the faces that flashed across screens at Christmas time.

However, after that brief glance Grant and Emily's direction, many of them looked at each other.

With their Cinderella shoes fitting perfectly, some of them didn't walk away.

A Cinderella Christmas

Epilogue

18 Months Later

"NO," Emily announced firmly.

"W-what?" Grant stuttered, his voice sounding strangled in his clear shock.

"No, Grant, I will not marry you." As if to reinforce her point, she removed her shaking hand from where it lay in his outstretched palm.

"I don't understand," Grant said shakily, still maintaining the position of kneeling on one knee as if he was merely waiting for the correct answer to drop from Emily's lips. "I thought... I mean..."

Emily groaned and put her hands over her eyes, wishing she could erase the memories of the last few minutes. "Why couldn't you have just waited until Friday?"

Grant's lips drew out in a straight line, and he staggered to his feet. "I specifically did not wait until Friday because I didn't want you to think that my proposal had anything to do with your accident case. It doesn't."

"Yes, it does! If I were to get sued and you married me before the case settled, then we could face needing to spend your money in lawyer's fees or a potential judgment against me."

Grant shook his head stubbornly. "I love you, and you love me. It shouldn't matter!"

"It matters to me," Emily replied, matching his stubbornness in full measure.

"Are you saying that if you happen to be sued in the next forty-eight hours, you don't plan on marrying me at all?"

Grant seemed angry, but couldn't he understand that it was tearing her up and that she was trying to protect him?

"I can't marry you. I don't want you to be liable for any of my potential debt."

"I don't care! There isn't a price tag on getting to be your husband. Emily, any amount of money would be worth it."

"I'm sorry, Grant. I can't do it. I simply can't allow someone else to take that kind of punishment for me."

"Is that what you tell Jesus? Will you not allow Him to make the sacrifice for you either?"

Emily looked at Grant steadily, clearly communicating the hurt he'd just inflicted. Then she turned and walked back down the path to her car.

It had all been so perfect. Grant had asked her to meet him for an evening walk around the lake. The summer temperature was warm but not too hot, the breeze off the lake cooling it just enough to be perfect. When they'd reached a place where a field of wildflowers met the water, Grant had dropped on one knee and spoken beautiful words of how he loved her and loved the way she challenged and inspired him. Then he'd asked her to marry him.

And she'd had to say no.

"Emily, wait!" Grant said, coming up the path behind her. "I'm sorry. I shouldn't have said that."

Emily stopped and nodded, though she still couldn't look at him.

"Emily, I've wanted to ask you to marry me for a very long time, but I know you've still been nervous about the accident and a potential lawsuit. I finally decided to go ahead and ask you before the two-year mark because I specifically wanted you to know that whatever your future is, I intend to be in it. No matter what. The accident is not a big deal to me. I believe God brought us together and that He will be faithful regardless of what the future holds. I didn't realize that you don't intend to marry me at all if things don't turn out the way you want."

"I appreciate that sentiment, Grant, but I still wish you had waited. I am not sane enough right now to answer such a question."

"Emily, it's been a year and a half since we met. I've tried to take things slow, but the reality is that I've wanted to marry you since before I knew your name. I love you, and I thought you loved me, too. But if there is a set of circumstances that exist where you don't want to marry me, then I'm not sure where that leaves us. For me, there is no circumstance that would change my desire to be with you always as your husband."

Emily shook her head, too choked up to answer. She honestly had no idea where that left them either. Was he breaking up with her?

Grant sighed and ran a hand through his hair in frustration.

"I'll know more on Friday," Emily said weakly.

"I'm not sure Friday will work for me," Grant whispered tiredly.

Emily nodded. She understood. He wanted to know that her love for him wasn't dependent on circumstances, and she didn't know that she could give him that assurance. Not because she didn't love him, but because with the two-year mark of her accident forty-eight hours away, everything was being filtered through fear. What Grant didn't understand was that her motivation in saying 'no' was to protect him. She didn't want his life ruined because of her. She loved him too much to do that to him.

"I have some more letters for you at the car," Grant said. "I'll give them to you, and then I need to run to pick Mila up at softball practice."

Emily followed him to his car, and he gave her three envelopes before sliding into the driver's seat.

"I'll see you later," Emily said as he started his engine.

Grant didn't respond but instead sent her a long look that clearly communicated both the depth of his love and the depth of his pain—pain that she had caused.

Emily drove to her parents' house and took a moment to collect herself. She needed to put on her best acting façade in front of her parents in order to pretend that everything was fine. They had invited her to dinner and couldn't back out now. But she didn't feel up to talking to them, especially when she knew they would probably side with Grant. Her parents adored her boyfriend and would be upset if they felt Emily hadn't treated him fairly.

With a deep breath, Emily grabbed the letters, stuck them in her purse, and carried the whole thing inside.

No sooner had she greeted Sparkles with a thorough pet and sat at the counter than her dad came up beside her and pointedly nudged her phone closer from where she had set it on the smooth counter surface.

"Why don't you give him a call?"

"Give who a call?" Emily asked, startled at the thought that Grant may have already called and tattled that she'd refused his proposal.

"Give your lawyer a call," Peter said, wiggling his

eyebrows expectantly.

Emily shook her head adamantly. "No, why would I do that? If I call him, I will be charged for the call and for him to review the case. If he starts making calls, then I'll be charged for those as well. Then, suddenly, everyone will start realizing that Friday is the deadline, and they need to either sue me or get more money from me to settle the claim before time runs out."

"That doesn't seem likely that they could complete legal documents and get them filed before 5:00 Friday," Peter said skeptically.

"Maybe they already have, and I just haven't received it. Theoretically, if they file at 4:58 Friday, I may not be notified of it until next week. Maybe notification is already in the mail."

"Then call the insurance agent and ask him about the claim."

Emily shook her head, unwilling to do that either. "The same reasons still exist for not calling him. I don't want someone calling around and asking questions this close to the deadline."

"Emily, this is ridiculous. You should call. Your fears aren't exactly rational. What the other party intends to do is already done, and finding that out doesn't matter at this point."

Emily stubbornly refused. "I'll call on Friday. Not before."

"Tell me again. What was the last you heard from the lawyer?" Emily's mom asked worriedly, looking up from where she was rolling out biscuit dough.

"I heard from him four months ago. He'd talked, repeatedly, to the other driver and her husband. They said they wanted $20,000 from me even though all of her medical expenses were paid, her car was replaced, and they had another $60,000 to put as cash directly into their account. Apparently, they felt the limits offered by my insurance aren't enough. My lawyer explained that I am a teacher and don't have that much disposable money to pay. I gave him the okay to offer them

$2500 as a token to get the claim settled. He said he'd talk to them and get back to me, but I never heard anything after that."

"And you didn't follow up with him because to do so would cost you even more money," Kim surmised.

"Yes," Emily nodded. "Just the work he did with talking to the other party and to me four months ago was over a thousand dollars."

"Emily, I will pay the bill if you give someone a call right now," her dad said irritably.

"Dad, I appreciate that, but I'm not going to call. It's too big of a risk when we'll find out in just a couple days."

"I don't see it as a risk. What's done is done at this point."

"Dad, you told me yourself just last week that you thought they were going to sue me."

Peter winced. "I shouldn't have said that. I just thought that since you hadn't heard anything, the only reasonable explanation is that they were preparing to file suit. At this point, however, you've waited long enough. Either they are, or they aren't, and I think you should find out. You said yourself that you may not know until next week. What if the papers are in the mail or you don't get served until after the weekend?"

"I'll call on Friday," Emily promised. "If I don't hear anything before then, I'll call the insurance guy in charge of the claim on Friday."

While not happy, Emily's parents settled for that answer. They ate dinner and Emily helped with the dishes afterward. They asked if Emily wanted to stay and watch a movie. After all, summer's schedule was a lot more doable since Emily didn't need to be to work early in the morning. But Emily was emotionally exhausted. She felt her mask slipping, and it wouldn't be long until her parents understood that she was very upset about something.

Retrieving her purse off the counter, she stopped when she saw the two envelopes sticking out the top. Curious, she took them out and slid her finger down the seam to break the seal. Each of the letters was addressed to "Cinderella at *The Brighton Daily*." Though it wasn't surprising, it still gave Emily a thrill. Even a year and a half after Grant's article about her came out, she still received mail addressed to the mysterious Cinderella. The article had gone viral by any standard, the public response being so profound that the newspaper finally agreed to accept mail on behalf of the woman who wished to remain anonymous.

Grant had been successful at keeping her identity hidden, though it had been difficult. A few times, other networks had figured it out by the simple fact that she and Grant were spending time together. Fortunately, reporters had checked to confirm with the paper before releasing the information, and the newspaper had been able to convince them that leaving the mystery intact was in the best interest of everyone.

By this point, the amount of mail for Cinderella had decreased dramatically, but Emily still occasionally received letters from around the world telling Cinderella how her story had changed individual lives and thanking her.

Emily pulled the single piece of paper from one of the envelopes and read,

Dear Cinderella,

Thank you for the shoes. I've tried to wear them well in both little and big things. I have a friend who has been going through a lot of depression. Honestly, she is a very draining, negative person to be around, and a lot of her friends have simply gotten tired and moved on. The other day, after I saw another of her gloomy posts, I remembered that I hadn't talked to her in a long time. We're actually more acquaintances than friends anyway, and it really shouldn't have bothered me. But it did. Remembering Grant Dillon's article about you, I went ahead and texted her, even though I didn't want to. I asked her how she was and talked to her for a while. A few days later, she called and thanked me. She said that she'd decided in her heart that she was going to commit suicide the day she'd made that social media post. Because of my text, she realized that people really did care for her and changed her mind. My friend has a long way to go, and I'm trying to get her help that she desperately needs, but the reason she is alive today is because I wore your shoes that day.

Thank you,
Janelle Morison

With tears in her eyes, Emily quickly drew out the other letter.

Dear Cinderella,

I just wanted to tell you what an impact your story has had on my life. My seven-year-old daughter has cancer. My husband left us a couple of years ago, so it's just me needing to shoulder a seemingly impossible task. My life was pretty much at a stand-still, and because our future was full of fear, I was even afraid to breathe. Grant Dillion's article eighteen months ago changed my life. I realized that God didn't want me to just endure. Even though I faced horrible circumstances, God still intended to use me. I started living again, letting both my future and my daughter's rest in His hands while working to see and bless those on the sidelines of our lives. The good news is that my daughter is currently in remission, but not completely out of the woods. Though I don't know what tomorrow will bring, because of your story, I have faith that God will be there and will use me in the meantime until then.

Thank you,
Kara Drew

Emily finished reading, stuffed each letter back into its envelope, and rushed to the door.

"Emily, what's wrong?" Kim called in alarm.

"I just figured out what a complete hypocrite I am," she said, throwing the door open to the sight of the setting sun.

"Where are you going?" Peter asked, obviously confused.

"I need to get to the dollar store before they close. I need to buy a notebook."

"EMILY, I'm so glad you're here!" Mila gushed, throwing her arms around Emily as soon as she opened the door.

"Of course!" Emily answered. "I told you I would."

"Yes, but then Dad said you two had a disagreement, and then I was worried… Nevermind. You're here, and that's what matters. That and my hair. Alexis's mom is going to be here to pick me up for the youth outing in thirty minutes. Do you think that's enough time to fix this?" Mila pointed to hair that would do an '80s punk rocker proud.

"Yes, I can," Emily said with more confidence than she felt.

Not even bothering with asking how Mila's hair got in such condition, she quickly sat the 15-year old on a chair in the kitchen, heated a curling iron, and began working magic.

Mila kept a constant monologue, checking Emily's progress in a hand-held mirror.

On the one hand, Emily didn't quite understand why Mila insisted on such an elaborate hairstyle for a youth group hike and bonfire. On the other hand, she remembered what it was like to be fifteen-going-on-sixteen, and when Mila asked her earlier in the week to come help, she had readily agreed.

"Where's your dad?" Emily asked casually, keeping her eyes on Mila's hair.

"He had to go to cover some event for the newspaper. Thankfully, Alexis's mom said she could pick me up. After your fight with dad, I was worried I would need to call Grandma to come help me get ready!"

Emily had hoped to get to talk to Grant while she was here, or at least deliver the notebook in person.

Covering the hairstyle with a final bit of spray, Emily pronounced her done.

"Thank you, Emily! I love it!" Mila said, studying herself in the mirror. After only a few seconds, however, her smile flexed into a scowl. "Do you think you can get me some of that lip gloss you use, next time you buy some for yourself? Dad says I can wear a little makeup, but I don't know what to wear."

Emily reached into her purse and drew out a small tube. "It's yours, Mila. I saw you liked it last week, so I asked your dad if it would be okay and bought you your own lip gloss. Maybe this weekend I can come over, and you can see how you like some of my other makeup."

Mila threw her arms around Emily once again and was blubbering so much that they almost couldn't get her lip gloss in the right place.

"Mila, can you do me a favor?" Emily asked once they had everything settled. "Can you give this notebook to your dad when you get home tonight?"

"Oh, sure!" Mila said distractedly as she busily made fish faces into the mirror, inspecting her lips with the new gloss.

Recognizing that her words may not have made it through to actual understanding, Emily hesitantly left the notebook on the counter, hoping that if Mila didn't mention it, Grant would still spot it.

As she did eighteen months ago, Emily left a notebook for Grant to find. Only this time, leaving it was very deliberate.

WITH her heart beating erratically, Emily dialed the numbers on her phone at 4:45 in the afternoon, exactly two years after she'd caused a car accident.

"May I speak with Andy Schultz, please?" Emily asked breathlessly.

"Andy isn't in right now, but can I help you with something?" the friendly voice on the other end asked.

Emily cleared her throat and readjusted the phone in her sweaty palm. "I… um… I was just wanting to check the status of a claim. Today marks two years since my accident, and I haven't heard that it was settled."

"I can check that for you to try to see what's going on," the woman assured. "Do you have a claim number?"

Emily rattled off the number she had written carefully on an index card held ready in her hand.

The silence stretched as the woman looked up the information, and Emma literally shook with the adrenaline coursing through her veins. She was at least thankful that she was home alone when she made this call. Though her parents had called at least five times today to see if she'd heard anything, Emma had made herself wait until fifteen minutes before the close of the day. She knew on some level that it was ridiculous fear, but that stroke of the clock was in some way symbolic. She had waited two years. She wasn't going to cheat now.

"It looks like all the papers were signed and the claim settled on April 12 of this year."

"W-What?" Emma stammered.

"The other party signed papers accepting the limits of the insurance pay-out and agreeing not to hold any further liability against you," the woman explained factually.

Emma swallowed. They'd signed it. She hadn't had to pay anything more, and they'd signed it.

"April 12?" her voice quavered. "That was over two months ago! Why wasn't I notified?"

She had just spent considerable time alternately making herself sick with worry and praying fervently for a prayer God had already answered two months before.

Forgive me, Lord. Yet again, I should have trusted you

more!

"I was never notified," Emily said quietly. "Never by phone call or by mail."

"Well, that's strange," the agent murmured as if looking for something. "There isn't a note saying we notified you, but that's our usual practice. I see you have a lawyer on file here. Do you want me to notify him?"

"I guess," Emily said, trying to figure out if it would cost her more money to notify him or not. She certainly didn't want him charging her to work on a closed case. "As long as he doesn't charge me another fee for closing the file."

"I can also send you a copy of the signed agreement," the agent offered helpfully.

"I would appreciate that." Maybe actually seeing the document would make it seem real.

"I'm not sure what to say about you not being notified sooner," the insurance agent finally concluded. "Sorry."

Emily appreciated the sentiment, but "sorry" seemed woefully inadequate right now.

Two months. All of her prayers for the past two years were answered in a miracle that happened while she wasn't looking.

With nothing more to say, Emily hung up with the insurance agent and sat in silence for a solid five minutes, simply staring at the wall in front of her.

She had been a caged bird for so long, now that the cage was gone, she didn't realize she could fly away. It all felt so unreal. She didn't feel much different than she had mere minutes ago. She should be overjoyed, and yet she was just numb.

It was over, and yet she didn't know what to do.

Suddenly, she remembered and stood up, grabbing her keys.

"Yes, I do," she whispered. "I know exactly what to do!"

She turned the doorknob and threw open the door to find Grant standing there with arm raised as if to knock.

"Hi," he greeted hesitantly.

"Hi," Emily responded.

He held out the notebook in his hand toward Emily. "Does this mean what I think it means?"

Oh, how she loved him! The eager nervousness marking his face wasn't because he anxiously wanted to know what happened with the accident claim. He didn't care. He wanted her no matter what the circumstances.

And she wanted him.

"I was wrong when I answered your question the other day," Emily explained quietly, accepting the notebook. "Later that night, I realized that faith and love should be independent of circumstances and that if God wanted us together, He fully intends to be with us through every circumstance in all our tomorrows. I thought that was a lesson I'd already learned, but apparently not."

She opened the notebook to the first page. On it was written the date from two days ago. The only other mark on the page was the word, "Yes."

"Two days ago, before I knew what would happen with the accident, I answered 'Yes.' Yes, I'll be your wife. And my answer for every day after that is also 'Yes,' no matter what."

She turned the page of the notebook. Very concisely, she stated the date written at the top and spoke the word, "Yes." Turning to the next page, she did the same thing. And the next page.

Emily paused briefly to insert in a musing voice, "I really don't think this notebook had enough pages." Then she continued, flipping each page, continuing to read the date and the word, "Yes," only to turn the page to the one marked with the next day's date, and announce the word, "Yes," again.

Grant's lips on hers silenced her speaking.

Complete joy raced through Emily, and she knew it had nothing to do with the insurance results. Instead, it had everything to do with the fact that she had trusted God enough to say "yes" two days ago. He had proved faithful two years ago, faithful two months ago, faithful two days ago, and she knew He'd be faithful whatever came their way tomorrow. No matter what "even ifs" happened, she knew God was in the business of giving beauty for ashes. After all, He'd turned her ashes into a beauty that He both shared with the world and provided a love she'd never imagined.

Lifting his head just a little, Grant released her only long enough to whisper, "Don't worry, Emily, I plan on buying you lots and lots more notebooks to fill."

Personal Note

IF anyone really wanted to know me, all they would need to do is read my books. Even though my books are all fiction, my heart and my experiences are written on every page. This book, in particular, is the most personal one I've ever written.

I was the person who watched a loved one suffer through Alzheimer's disease. I was the teacher who miscarried and still went to work to escape the grief. I was the mom looking longingly at a group of friends. I was the mom at the end of a long, chaotic day with kids. I was the girl sitting alone day after day in the lunchroom. I was the woman helplessly watching a horrible situation in a vet's office. I was the writer of a bunch of random words in an everything notebook. I was the woman crying on a corner who no one saw. And yes, I was the person who was at fault in an accident that hurt someone else. I am Emily. Every struggle and thought she had was first spoken in my own voice.

I wrote this book nearly a year ago as a way to help deal with my own issues following an accident where I, just like Emily, turned left on a blinking yellow light I thought was green. That day, I sat on the street corner and cried while people passed, not even one looking in my direction. Emily's story of anxiety is a mirror of my own, and like her, I also recognized myself in those who passed me on the street.

I am also the person who walked away.

The heartbreaking scene in the vet's office is near identical to one I actually witnessed. The differences are that I never found out what happened. I don't know if the old man paid for the injured dog's surgery or not. I don't know if the dog lived or died. The two men were at a standstill when I picked up my cat, turned around, and left the vet's office. I did not stop and pray with them like Emily did, and I will never know if that was an opportunity I missed because, on that day, I walked away.

There are countless examples of almost daily instances where I don't see or simply ignore a prompting of kindness with the exact excuses offered by the characters in this book. I'm too busy. It would be too weird. The person doesn't actually need my help. I don't always respond to texts when I should. I scroll on by a social media post without letting a person in pain know I care. In both little and big things, it is more convenient to watch from a distance rather than go through the potential discomfort of doing something. It's not even deliberate. Most of the times, I'm so wrapped in my own world, that I simply don't notice where I may do something kind for someone.

It's a very strange experience to have your own book convict you. Writing out my feelings through Emily helped me deal with the trauma of what had happened, but it also gave me a new outlook on life. Since I sat on the street corner, I've tried to notice others. I try to live by the idea, *"When it is an act of kindness, there should only ever be one answer to the question of "maybe I should."* The answer should always be "Yes."

In simple little things, I've tried to recognize God's nudging and minister to others the way He would have me. From baking cookies to texting someone to simply not being satisfied with an "I'm fine," I've tried to be better at seeing those on my own sidelines. Like the character I created, if I can help it, I never want anyone else to experience crying on a corner with no one who sees. I'm certainly a work in progress, and I'm sure I still probably miss opportunities more often than I take them, but my prayer is that God shows me those who need kindness and help me to not walk away.

The Christmas Card series is probably my most inspirational. Their message is meant to be enjoyed and shared, leaving a positive imprint on the world. When I first wrote, *The Christmas Card,* I intended that it be just that—a shareable card that could inspire and bring Christmas joy. This second book in the series is no different. Please share both the book and the message of *A Cinderella Christmas* with others. The greatest compliment you can ever give an author is a recommendation, either through a review or through personally telling others. I can't wait to see what God does with this message, and if you are a part of His work in that area, you have my sincere thanks.

I hope this book changes your Christmas in ways that extend beyond December 25. I've certainly tried to wear the Cinderella shoes well, and my sincere hope is that you will try them on, too. My prayer is that this story will touch you and change you in a way that in turn changes the world.

God, help us to not walk away.

Discussion Questions

THIS is a tough Reader's Guide to write! *A Cinderella Christmas* is filled with such spiritual depth that narrowing it down to a few sparse questions would never quite do it justice or encompass the full message. What spoke to you most in the story may not be what meant the most to your neighbor. The part that resonated with you and your experience most may be completely different than what touched someone else. Fortunately, much of the themes, messages, emotions, and characters are universal in that everyone should come away with something that touched them and made them think. It just isn't likely to be the same thing!

That's why sharing is so important! Your thoughts about this book may very much bless someone else, both through your own words and actions. If your preference would be to simply go chapter by chapter and discuss what was meaningful to you in each, then go for it. If, however, you'd rather have discussion questions to start the conversation, the following is my feeble and in no way exhaustive, attempt. Most importantly, you should come away from this book changed. My prayer is that this story spoke to you and changed your perspective in a way that glorifies God. Share what you got out of this book with others.

Don't leave the Cinderella shoes behind. They are meant to be worn by you. Put them on and take a look around to see who you can bless today.

---

1. Have you ever experienced something traumatic or wrestled with the guilt from a mistake like Emily experienced?

How was Emily's experience the same or different than your own? How did you handle it?

1 Peter 5:7, Jonah 2:2, Philippians 3:13-15, Psalm 33:20-22

2. How would Emily's life or the lives of others have been different if God had prevented Emily's accident?

How would your own life be different if God had spared you from your difficult circumstances? Can you now see any recognizable lesson God taught you through that experience?

Proverbs 19:21, Romans 8:28, Psalm 37:23-24, Jeremiah 29:11

3. Which character in the book did you relate to the most? Did you recognize any of their situations or emotions as ones you have experienced?

4. How did Emily learn to trust God even with her uncertain future? How did you deal with your own life in limbo and uncertainty?

Psalm 32:8, Matthew 6 31-33, Isaiah 43:2

5. One of the wonderful things about books is that you get to find out the ending. But life usually isn't so convenient and requires times of stressful waiting. A big theme of this book includes learning to trust that God is good in spite of your circumstances and uncertainty. When have you felt in limbo in your own life, needing to wait before knowing how something would end?

Isaiah 43:1-3, Philippians 3:13-15, Matthew 6:26

6. Have you ever felt like Emily did when sitting at the corner crying while everyone walked past? Have you ever been on the sidelines wishing someone would notice you? Tell about the time, your feelings, and how you reacted.

7. Tell of a time when you noticed someone on the sidelines of your life, stopped, and helped. What were the results?

Tell of a time when you walked away. What opportunity might you have missed out on?

8. How do you know when God is nudging you to do something? In the book, Emily writes about the idea that if something occurs to you to do and the motivation is kindness, the answer should always be yes. What do you think of that idea?

Ephesians 2:10, Philippians 2:1-14, 1 John 3:17, Acts 20:35, Matthew 25-34-36

9. Both Grant and Mila experienced some unpleasant consequences to their acts of kindness. Have you ever had an act of kindness not go well?

2 Thessalonians 3:13, Matthew 5:11, Matthew 5:43-48

10. Tell of a time when you didn't walk away, saw someone, and did something small or big to help?

John 13:34-35, 1 Thessalonians 3:12

11. Tell of a time when you thought maybe you should do something, but talked yourself out of it and walked away?

Proverbs 24:16, Psalm 37:23-24, Lamentations 3:22-23, Hebrews 6:10, Matthew 23:11

12. What scene in the book touched you the most or was your favorite?

13. What message in the book impacted you the most? Did you find anything personally convicting?

How do you anticipate applying that message to your life?

Luke 6:38, Matthew 6:33, 1 Peter 4:10, Romans 12:9-13, 1 Corinthians 10:31

Excerpt: Under the Christmas Star

PLEASE enjoy this brief excerpt from Under the Christmas Star, available now.

EMMA tapped her fingers on the hard surface of the steering wheel. Starting at her pinky fingers, she tapped the corresponding fingers of both hands until they counted up to her thumbs. Then she reversed and counted back down to her pinky fingers, only to repeat the ritual all over again.

She hated being late. It tied her nerves up in knots worse than those found when unraveling last year's Christmas lights.

She breathed in and out.

In for the space of five tapping fingers. Out for the space of five.

And again.

Years of training should make managing her challenges

easier, yet Emma Sheldon couldn't make it through a day without heavily leaning on the techniques taught to her as a "special" child. Even now, her steadily tapping fingers and slow, practiced breathing were the only things keeping her focused on the angry red light taunting her from above her windshield.

Emma risked a glance down at the clock before shooting it back up to the light. She told herself she still had plenty of time to drop the ornaments off at church and make it to the post office to mail the other boxes before the 5:00 close. If only Brooke's uncle, Wayne, hadn't shown up and ordered a custom ornament right as she was packing up to leave the Out of the Blue Bouquet, then maybe time wouldn't be so short.

As soon as the irritable thought crossed her mind, Emma winced, knowing that it wasn't quite accurate. Brooke was kind enough to let Emma sell ornaments on consignment at her florist shop, and Emma could never be anything but grateful to get a custom order.

The real fault for her running late belonged long before delivering ornaments to the shop. If she hadn't wasted so much time obsessively sorting and packing the ornaments, then she could have had time to spare to run all her errands. Unfortunately, facing the consequences due to her obsessive tendencies wasn't unfamiliar territory either. As always, every task presented the challenge of trying to find a balance between allowing herself to be quirky Emma while fighting against losing herself in the lonely world of her own mind, and this time, she had obviously come out uneven on the balance scales.

The light finally turned green, and Emma put steady pressure on the gas pedal to drive through the intersection. Even though time was short, she could never allow herself to inch beyond the 35-mph posted speed limit.

Fortunately, downtown Crossroads boasted a total of only two stoplights, and Emma managed to hit the second one green. Three minutes later, she pulled into the church parking lot and found a space on the end of a row. The lot was empty but for a few cars, and still, Emma stayed true to her natural tendency and parked away from everyone else.

She hurriedly snatched her purse from the passenger seat and checked that her phone was nestled inside for safekeeping. With movements quick and agitated, she drew the long purse strap over her neck to hang across her body, only to unintentionally pin her long reddish-brown curls beneath the taut strap. Unable to handle the discomfort, she tried to reverse her movements and take the purse strap off, but the limited space in the driver's seat only succeeded in knocking her elbows and head against the window in her efforts.

She pushed open the door and unfolded her tall, slender frame out of the car. With a few more contortions, she finally pulled her hair out from under the purse strap only to decide that it still made too much of a hangman's noose for her comfort. She yanked the strap off her neck, wrapped it around the purse, and stuck the entire thing under her elbow to carry.

Breathing heavily with the effort of her gyrations, she pulled the lever to release the hatch of her SUV and glanced nervously at the sky. Evening in late November came early, and by the time she finished at the post office, she'd be forced to deal with the glare of headlights on the drive home. She didn't enjoy driving in the middle of the day with all the sights and sounds threatening to overwhelm her senses, but driving at night, with the added contrast of darkness and bright lights, only made the experience more overwhelming.

Emma scurried around to the back of her 1997 Honda Civic hatchback, worriedly noting that the two other cars parked close to the church entrance. The ladies on the church decorating committee insisted that they needed the ornaments today in order to decorate before Sunday's church service. If given a choice, Emma would have never ventured out on Black Friday. The thought of braving the crowds sent her anxiety rising. However, some of the ladies insisted that Emma make the delivery today so they could get it done tonight and still keep tomorrow's shopping plans. Not wanting to draw attention to herself or explain why the day following Thanksgiving was not a good day for her, Emma bravely agreed.

Setting her purse down, she pulled one of the boxes out of the back and opened it to make sure she selected the correct one. Seeing that it was one of the boxes destined for the post office and not the church, she moved to push it back and pull out the other one, chiding herself that she had switched the box's positions from their intended positions when loading. However, before the lid folded back on itself, she couldn't help but notice several of the ornaments shifted from their neat rows.

Unable to resist fixing the problems, Emma pulled out a glass ornament and carefully repaired its nest in the box. She picked up the delicate bauble to replace it in safety and couldn't help but see the imperfections that, to her, seemed glaringly obvious. She wavered, wondering whether or not she should even include the flawed ornament in the shipment to the gift shop. Glass blowing was one of her more recent art mediums, and she wasn't yet confident in her artistic expertise.

No, she chided herself, forcing her fingers to replace the ornament. *Everyone does not share my standards for perfection. I've already prayed for the recipient of that ornament, and I won't grab that prayer back from God's capable hands.*

However, despite her pep talk, she couldn't resist repeating that prayer, just in case God didn't hear the first time or she hadn't remembered to pray the right words. Even as she thought it, she knew her reasoning was silly, but she couldn't help trying for a redo, just in case.

Lord, please help this ornament, and all of my ornaments be a blessing to the people who give them homes. Help the owner of this glass ornament see past the imperfections to recognize its beauty, and somehow let that be a reminder that you love them, no matter their own mistakes.

Her finger found a slight irregularity in the glass, and she studied how the fading light created a soft prism effect out of what was technically a mistake. This was the ornament she had dubbed "starry night." The blues and streaks of yellow blurred in such a way to remind her of Van Gough's famous painting. Even though she didn't always care for the style, she'd always been rather partial to that painting because it, in turn, reminded her of what the sky must have looked like when the angels appeared to the shepherds to announce Jesus's birth.

Yet, in spite of her observations about the beauty of the light through the glass and the fact that she loved the ornament, Emma still found herself wishing she could have a redo on more than just the prayer. Her heart's desire was that this ornament would hang on the tree of someone who didn't have a relationship with Christ and that, in seeing it, the person would somehow see what Emma saw. Oh, that someone could have a starry night experience that Emma's ornament inspired!

Ridiculous. Emma knew it was ridiculous. There's no way someone could see Christmas through her flawed ornament. After all, no one saw the world the same way as Emma in any other facet of life. Though she felt assured that God's purpose could cover her work's inadequacies, she really wished it didn't have to. How much more could God use better quality handiwork?

Promising herself she would do better next time, Emma replaced the ornament and rearranged a few more. Her movements paused as she held a glass ball ornament with an exquisite purple and green strand of flowers inside and couldn't remember which row it belonged in. Had she previously sorted it into the row with the clear and white ornaments or in the row with the other purple ones?

Her gaze studied the box and she felt a familiar sensation of nausea. She had done it wrong. She shouldn't have sorted the ornaments based on color. Maybe she should have sorted based on shape, or media, or even theme. She could put all the nativity ornaments in one row, or maybe she should separate the glass and ceramic ones.

She shut her eyes against the swirling colors of ornaments. Reaching out her fingers to the edge of the car, she found the hard surface and began tapping her fingers down to 1 and back up to 5. If only her mom was here. Just hearing words to bring the rest of reality into Emma's small sphere would help. She knew the organization didn't matter to everyone else, but it mattered to her. And in her mind, it really should matter to everyone else as well.

Of course, none of this would be a problem if Emma's parents had been in town. Emma's mom could have chauffeured Emma around for her errands, greatly diminishing Emma's anxiety level from the beginning. However, Emma's parents had left early that morning to visit her brother, and because of Emma's business commitments, she'd needed to stay home.

Managing for a few days by herself really shouldn't be an issue. After all, Emma was twenty-seven years old and a successful business owner. She should be able to handle her own affairs and run her own errands. She needed to do it herself, and perhaps more importantly, she wanted to do it herself. She was a smart, capable adult. She could do this.

With a deep fortifying breath, Emma opened her eyes and resolutely nestled the disputed ornament in between the red and blue rows and forced herself to shut the box lid.

She pulled the box on the right with determination, eagerly muzzling the wayward thoughts challenging her competency. Everything was under control now.

If only the daylight didn't disappear so very quickly. Nervousness lapped at the edges of the dwindling light, disputing that she held control as captive as she wanted to believe.

Emma hefted the box into her arms. She hoped the ornaments she'd selected met with the committee's approval. Maybe if she explained the reasons for her selections, they would understand. But what if they didn't? What if she hadn't chosen the right ornaments? What if they just weren't good enough?

"Get down!" the growl came from behind Emma.

Startled, she jerked around to find who was speaking. "W-What?"

"Get down!" came the order again.

Three men confronted her, the bottom half of their faces covered with kerchiefs.

Emma shook her head in confusion, not understanding the order. What did "get down" mean? Did they want her to set her box down?

Fear strangled her, and she didn't know what to do. Who were these men? What did they want?

Something flashed in the waning light. The gun lifted into firing position before Emma realized what it was.

Instinctively, Emma reached out her hands in a defensive position toward the gun held by the figure in the center. "I don't under—"

Out of the corner of her eye, Emma saw the figure on the left jerk suddenly. Emma flinched, lowering her head and turning as if to duck out of the way. Immediately, pain exploded in Emma's temple.

Her hands relinquished their burden, the box slipping gently from her limp fingers. With a whimper, Emma collapsed into darkness with the shattering of ornaments the last sound she heard.

Find the latest information and connect with Amanda at her website: **www.amandatru.com**

THE CHRISTMAS CARD Series:

The Christmas Card

A Cinderella Christmas

YESTERDAY Series:

Yesterday

The Locket

Today

The Choice

Tomorrow

The Promise

Forever (coming soon)

TRU EXCEPTIONS Series:

Baggage Claim

Mirage

Point of Origin

Rogue

CROSSROADS Series:
Out of the Blue Bouquet
Yesterday's Mail
Under the Christmas Star
Betwixt Two Hearts (coming soon)

CROSSROADS SUSPENSE Series:
The Night of the White Elephant

BRIDES BY MAIL Series:
(Written with Cami Wesley)
Bride of Pretense
Bride by Request
Bride of Regret

THE SECRET BRIDE SOCIETY Series:
The Secret Bride Society

Christian Romance:
Secret Santa
The Random Acts of Cupid
The Assumption of Guilt
The Christmas Card

Clean Romance:
The Romance of the Sugar Plum Fairy

Children's:
Under the pen name J. Lasterday

DOG THE DRAGON series:
The Dragon's Escape
The Cabin Boy's Treasure
The Great Expedition

About the Author

AMANDA TRU loves to write exciting books with plenty of unexpected twists. She figures she loses so much sleep writing the things, it's only fair she makes readers lose sleep with books they can't put down!

Amanda has always loved reading, and writing books has been a lifelong dream. A vivid imagination helps her write captivating stories in a wide variety of genres. Her current book list includes everything from historical, to action-packed suspense, to inspirational romance, to a Christian time travel/romance series. Amanda is also the author and organizer behind the unique, multi-author Crossroads collection series.

Amanda is a former elementary school teacher who now spends her days being mommy to her four young children and her nights furiously writing. Amanda and her family live in a small Idaho town where the number of cows outnumbers the number of people.